Carsten Je[...]

He has wor[...]

and at *Det [...]*

editor of the [...] magazine *[...]* from 1985

to 1990. *Earth in the Mouth* is his first book to

be translated into English.

earth
in
the
mouth

a story

CARSTEN JENSEN

translated from

the danish

by

Anne Born

PICADOR

First published 1994 by Picador

a division of Pan Macmillan Publishers Limited
Cavaye Place London SW10 9PG
and Basingstoke

Associated companies throughout the world

ISBN 0 330 33147 7

Originally published 1991 as *Jorden i munden, En fortælling*
by Samleren, Copenhagen.

9 8 7 6 5 4 3 2 1

A CIP catalogue record for this book is available from
the British Library

Phototypeset by Intype, London
Printed by Cox & Wyman Ltd, Reading, Berkshire

one

Sometimes I imagine I'm back in India. Again I'm walking beside the river with its burning funeral pyres, where I once saw a foot melt like a wax candle. It's myself I want to meet. It's a moment of great significance for me.

But my imagination amplifies in an odd way, which I don't understand and have no control over. There's an old man, he forces himself on me. He is bent and crooked with age. In a quavering voice he confidentially imparts a flood of details about the river, the symbolism in the colours of the grave clothes or the buildings around us. The English formed by his black bloodless lips is almost incomprehensible, a hoarse hawking in which the sentences run on with no pause between words. I wave him away with my hand when he comes to a full stop by stretching out his hand and begging for baksheesh. He bends down, picks up a stone from the river bank and threatens me with it. I laugh at him. Then he launches himself at me and seizes my arm. In a rage that erupts like an explosion as unexpected to myself as to him, I lunge out at him and hit him on the shoulder. I will not allow a stranger to touch my body.

The blow knocks the ancient's feet from under him. He huddles on the ground in humiliation, as if waiting to be kicked.

3

I remember another kick from long ago, and at that moment I recognize the pattern of lines on his forehead that once reminded me of a map. It has grown darker with the years, I see.

I don't know why I should be haunted by this image. Why should I have this urge to picture to myself the fearful straits to which life can reduce a human being?

Is it revenge or reverence?

The horn in the buffalo's brain?

The Indian landscape is astonishingly monotonous. One small plot succeeds another. Even the palms stand dusted over with the same sand colour as the earth. Now and again a clay-yellow river breaks the monotony with its irregular, winding course. On the banks the women dry their saris, and the water-buffalo stand in water up to their knees, while the dried mud on their black backs crackles in the sun. Dawn is heralded by the smell of excrement. Those in need crawl up the slopes banking the railway line and relieve themselves with their backs to the passing passengers. Their bare rumps seem black in the early light and the turds take on a threatening, indistinct dark shape like shadows grown out of the earth or perhaps holes of indeterminate depth.

The train journeys when I sat in the open doorway with my feet resting on the footboard held a monotony that had a kind of healing effect on me and finally became a part of my body. The thudding of the rail joints reverberated in my brain like an endless tally of numbers which, when you have first started with number one, you need never again stop counting. You have secured a share in eternity.

The unvarying landscape, the hot wind in the open door of the carriage, the rail joints counting for me.

It is a perilous recollection.

It still holds me prisoner.

There's this story about the apostle who landed on the Malabar Coast. Even before he had walked out of the surf he was surrounded by Hindus asking him about his God and begging him to prove the existence of his God by a miracle. When he said he would take a handful of water and throw it into the air, where the drops would stay up there hanging, they laughed at him and encouraged him to do it. The apostle made a scoop out of his hands. Then he threw the water up over his head, and lo! the drops spread out, but they did not fall, they stayed there hanging and sparkling in the sun, while they proved the truth of his words. And the Hindus fell to their knees in the foaming surf and allowed themselves to be converted, and he baptized them then and there.

And I am sure that, with their heads underwater, they went on laughing at the apostle, whom they had lured into playing his stupid games with gravity even before he had felt their soil under his feet.

I remember my homecoming too. I left the autostradas and crossed the border one night in May just after midnight. There was nothing left of my chest except the ribs and I had the feeling that the wind went right through me as if I were an aeolian harp. I had to walk the last ten kilometres. My appearance did not attract motorists. What I remember best were the kilometres on the signposts. Thirty-two kilometres to Kolding. Rather more to Fredericia. It was like coming home to a doll's house. It occurred to me, while walking along the hard shoulder, that I'd better be careful not to take overlong strides, for that would whisk me out of my own country again, past my life and my world, like rushing past a turning you haven't noticed.

Perhaps that is what happened. I went past.

I remember how enchanted you were, Thomas, by the fakirs, you had heard they had taught themselves to let their hearts beat only once in a minute. You thought that when they came to die it would be with an unused heart, not full of days but without having known the taste of days.

You thought of it with longing.

That is why we must wrestle with each other.

two

1

The world rotated, but not around him. It surged up and down in dizzy seasickness. It went at a whirling speed, and it stood stock-still. No power kept this wheel in motion other than the speed's own wildness and the rush of colours. There a face, there a back, then a cycle with spinning spokes like a small wheel in the middle of the big one, and again it spun round, like a sphere that stopped unexpectedly and started up in the opposite direction to its own course. He was obliged to lean backwards in order to find a fixed point in the firmament, but that too twisted and turned and tapered like a funnel or the base of a vortex.

Then the whirling stopped with a sound like canvas being ripped. There came a little voice, it was handed up to him. It lay in the pink palm of a hand and spoke. He didn't understand the words so he looked around for a mouth and a face, although the hand was speaking enough, stretched upwards, with the palm ready to be filled. Bigger than the biggest vessel was that hand, for it begged for his help. It sought the rarest raw material in the world, it sought salvation, and Thomas on his side prayed for help and searched for a face that could make all this comprehensible. He found a face filled with self-conscious childish sweetness, it met his gaze, and he assumed an air of incomprehension until the face put on a well-trained pathos with a mouth primed to the ugly folds of weeping, and then became imploring, frozen like one losing his grip over an abyss, and beneath all these expressions the face was merely indifferent, in routine expectation of the effect of its performance.

This took place a long way down, for the histrionic talent belonged to a child who ran along beside him. A freakish growth drove his height up above the houses and into another more distant firmament than that over this land. He walked on, on his enormous legs, but the child kept up with him on his, and he felt a thundering from the naked balls of feet against the earth. Then the child did something that started up the whirling again. It threw itself to its knees in front of him, slapped its palms, those little pink palms which had spoken earlier, on the ground. Now they were hidden, and the backs of the hands had to speak for them. Then the child lifted up its face and presented the final effect of its act, in which it annihilated all the others, even itself, and certainly him. The child kissed the toe of his boot with its little soft mouth, leaving behind a smear of saliva, something that happens to children in sleep or moments of great peace of mind. He stared, he couldn't believe it. The child would not move. It moved its mouth, but not away from the boot, just around on its surface, it did not lick, only the little lips kept on moving around as if to calculate how large the boot was. And the child's saliva flowed over the boot like an acid that made the leather dissolve. Its kiss burned his foot.

He wanted the child to move, but dared not touch it, as if he feared its brown skin was some sticky kind of flypaper. He tried to push the child gently away, as he would have a chewing puppy. But the child clasped the leg of his boot in a firm grip. He tried to take a step, but the child clung fast. It allowed itself to be dragged along on its naked stomach over the dirty pavement.

And the world rolled around them in huge, looping eddies.

He started to weep. He looked around for an adult who could release him from this terrible, incomprehensible thing. He had forgotten the fact that the child had merely begged for a coin and that everything that had happened between them until a moment before had precisely followed the well-rehearsed ritual between the beggar and the one forced to assume the role of benefactor. The child had forgotten this too. Its tears had led to a trembling that shook the whole of its small body. Together they wept noisily and desperately, the lad who had grown taller than the houses around him, and the ant on the toe of his boot.

The sun was about to set. The water from a nearby fountain created slow waves of fine spray, while the drops turned mellow in the red light of the sudden sunset. Then darkness fell like a door slammed shut. Shadows spread in the colonnade where the child had assailed him, broken here and there by the harsh light of fly-spotted fluorescent tubes. Faces emerged from the darkness into the cold light which neutralized colours and made the skin even darker than he had imagined it in Indians, umber bordering on black, the whites of eyes were yellow or red, mouths opened and shut, from behind the black lips shone a bloody glitter that reminded him of slaughtered animals.

He had an urge to kick. He shook his foot. He dared

11

not bend down and drag the small body from him, afraid that more fly papers would fuse them inseparably. Panic rose in him, the fear of becoming visible in the midst of the darkness of the colonnade and being caught in some unheard of action's projected light. Still, the kick was slowly approaching. He had to kick out at the child that was trying to make him bigger than he was. The kick did not come but it was as if in his foot, that until now had merely rocked symbolically as if to tell the ant there was no place for it on the toe of his boot, a new resolution was gathering.

And he would indeed have done it, the unheard of thing, would have kicked a child so it flew through the air, and would have remembered his kick with obvious shame and secret delight.

A brown hand, a large brown hand, suddenly enveloped the child's fragile upper arm in a firm grip and dragged it, with an ease Thomas envied, up from the ground and away from his boot. Then the child was briskly shaken, it dangled unresisting and routinely from the big hand, but grief still marked its face, concentrated into an ugly mask of suddenly advanced age. A voice scolded, then the hand released its grip. The child stood still for a moment, as if in shock, or perhaps considering a final appeal. Then it acknowledged defeat and ran off.

He stood there, staring at the suddenly empty toecap. He felt ashamed. He had done it again, behaved like a child. Self-reproach drummed on his skull, the aggression he had directed at the child a moment before now turned against himself, the other child, the most abject child, the blind passenger always searching for a hiding-place, a door others had opened, who must always be helped, who could do nothing by himself.

He came to himself when a friendly hand clapped him on the shoulder. It was the man who had come to his rescue, still standing beside him.

'Don't worry about it,' he said. 'It was nothing. Come, let us go and cool off in there.'

With a gesture of invitation he indicated a restaurant behind them. The whole scene had been enacted outside its windows. To his relief Thomas saw the blinds were drawn. Otherwise he would never have dared go in. He imagined the glances turned in his direction, the heads whispering together, he had to look down at his feet again and felt embarrassment take hold until it grew into the desire to die.

But this door, with the pompous brass rail across it, its imitation of a rare kind of wood and the letters announcing in a luminous reddish-orange that inside an air-conditioning plant rumbled away, that door was the hiding-place he always needed, it was the entrance to a darkness in which he could hide the uncertainty in his eyes and the shame he felt colouring his cheeks.

The sudden shift from heat to cold made him shudder. After the damp tropical heat the place was icy cold. The tears felt cold against his cheeks, and he rubbed his face. The restaurant was in almost total darkness, only small islands of light hovered over the tables. The faces and upper bodies of the diners were dramatically illuminated when they bent over their plates, then disappeared into the shadows again.

The stranger pulled out a chair for Thomas and sat down opposite him. He had a broad forehead in varying shades of gold and brown in a pattern reminiscent of a map, a strange effect which might have been due to the lighting.

His black hair was smooth and swept back, with high temples, it was a big face but reassuring, with none of the fierceness Thomas had found in the faces outside. The Indian reminded him of the father of a childhood friend, and he was seized with a strange feeling, as if he found himself in a *doppelgänger* world, where he would rediscover everything familiar to him from home, in a black mirror.

Then he realized where he had seen the Indian before. They had passed each other several times in the colonnade, which was built in a circle. He suddenly remembered the fairly short figure in a white nylon shirt and grey trousers and thought it odd that this very man should have fastened on him. A long-suppressed need to just give in and be trustful surged up in him. He felt as if a new bout of weeping was coming on.

The Indian passed him the menu. He took it, but asked for a cup of tea straight away. Strange food gave him the same feeling as a cage full of unknown animals. When he ordered a dish he felt as if he was putting his hand into the cage fearing all the time to be bitten. He would never have touched tea in the past. He had only learned to drink it during the journey. In the tea houses in Mashad and Herat they had served tea in little jar-shaped glasses with green mint leaves, which circulated in the amber-coloured liquid in slow spirals. It was the colours that had attracted him, and then the sugar, lying in a thick layer at the bottom of the glass.

The tea that was put before him was thick flowing, with milk, it had a flavour of cinnamon and cardamom. He took a gulp and felt it burning his throat. The cinnamon reminded him of rice pudding, which he hated, and he was afraid the milk would start forming a skin. He left the tea untouched after the first mouthful.

The Indian observed him from the other side of the table, as if he expected the effect of a magic potion. Then he leaned forward. His broad forehead came into the light, the strange irregular colour of the skin was still there. Black shadows ran from the corners of his eyes and fleshy nose.

'Yes,' he said, 'it's terror one feels, isn't it?' He was silent for a moment. 'Did you fly here?'

Thomas shook his head, unsure of the conversation.

'Terror,' repeated the Indian with unexpected vehemence and leaned even further forward with a jerk, until his broad forehead threatened to collide with the low-hung lamp.

'And sympathy,' he added quietly.

Thomas stiffened with embarrassment.

The Indian pushed his chair back and rose to his feet. The upper part of his body disappeared from the circle of light, only the waist with grey trousers and white shirt, bulging over his stomach, remained. His hand moved into the light, slightly clenched, with fingers together and thumb upwards, the skin was darker than his face.

'Forgive me,' came his voice from above in the darkness, 'I have forgotten to introduce myself. My name is George.' He laughed. 'No, it is not my name. It is something you would find completely unpronounceable. Unpronounceable.' He emphasized each single syllable and laughed again. 'But it reminds me of George.'

Thomas stretched out his hand and gave his name. He half rose but got wedged between the edge of the table and the chair, which he did not dare push back for fear of the noise it would make. He stood with his behind sticking out and half-bent knees, as if bowing.

'You are not hungry?' The stranger indicated the menu. Thomas shook his head and put his hand over the glass of tea as if he was afraid of being forced to drink it. The warm steam on the inside of his hand felt like a caress.

'Have you never been in an aeroplane?' George took up the earlier topic. Thomas nodded. 'Then you know. The sight of people from the air. Humanity. That's what I wanted to say, the sight of humanity from the air. Sometimes one must lift oneself up above the earth and see the whole thing at once.' He hesitated for a moment. 'I travel a great deal, you see.' He stopped and looked at Thomas, as if the last sentence had been the most important and everything that had preceded it merely a pretext.

'Once when I was coming home from America I sat beside a young lady. It was her first visit to India. Bombay appeared beneath us, and suddenly she began to cry. Out of terror. You know, an Indian city spreads out in all directions, it does not grow towards the sky like a town in the West, it rather resembles a camp of tents in a gale, with everyone clinging on to the earth and their scanty possessions. There you sit in the aeroplane, which is about to prepare for landing, you are still high up, and then you see these towns, stretching right out to the horizon, their extent is so huge that from your height in the air you can glimpse the curvature of the earth beneath the jumble of low houses and narrow streets. That is humanity, you think, I belong to that. You can take it in at a single glance. That is the

16

truth about what you are seeing, all the rest, the big cities of the West, the skyscrapers, motorways, airports, are mere stage props, behind them lies the earth with its immense curvature and its infinite masses of people, pressing themselves to it in terror. I understood that girl quite well. At that moment, when I saw humanity from above, I too felt like crying. We have bravely conquered gravity, but I don't think we have yet found the courage to endure the sight of ourselves.'

He uttered this after again vehemently leaning forwards. He grasped the edge of the table with both hands, his nose took a bearing on Thomas's tea glass, his whole face was in darkness, his forehead and the coarse dark hair stood out fully illuminated like a waxing moon slowly sailing over the table. Then he was back in his chair. He looked solemnly at Thomas. He had unctuously relished the words and rather declaimed than spoken them. His English was marked by the Hindu accent's rising and falling rhythm, which Thomas was inclined to find comical. But underneath that was a gentle, consoling melody that soothed him, it was that he listened to, not the words.

'My dear young friend,' said the other. 'I noticed you were weeping. Do not be ashamed of it. You should have been ashamed if you had not wept.'

He wagged his head loosely to and fro, that typical Indian movement that resembled a no but was a yes, or perhaps rather a word midway between them, a kind of goodwill, an admittance of mutual feeling in a world in which neither yea nor nay could be said, where there was neither rejection nor acceptance, but merely suffering and endurance. While he continued to wag he pursed his lips

17

in a smile. Thomas found the smile cloying, almost feminine, but he felt yet again that the smile was the same as the wagging head, it represented something midway between, neither man nor woman.

The Indian asked him about his travel plans. Thomas shook his head and then felt confused because he remembered the movement could have the opposite meaning. His embarrassment returned.

'I don't know India,' he said.

'Why are you travelling?'

Thomas thought for a long time. Then he said: 'There was a game I used to love when I was a child. In some of the magazines my mother took there was a page that was almost blank. The only thing printed on it was a lot of dots. Beside each dot was a number. You had to follow the numbers and draw a line from dot to dot. In the end it suddenly formed a horse and rider or perhaps something quite different. An invisible being had hidden itself in the paper. If you drew the lines properly you could entice it out. I think I'm travelling in the same way.'

He stopped. For a moment he thought he had said something stupid, but the Indian nodded at him encouragingly.

'You are an intelligent boy. I can hear you think about things.'

Thomas was not offended by this reference to his age. He was not a boy and he was not grown up, he was something in between, and that was why he was travelling, to cover the final stretch between the two points. He wanted to use the globe like a child who continually measures his height on the door frame.

But at this moment he wanted to be called a boy. He felt he was allowed that. It was a small breathing-space in the midst of the enormous stress of his journey.

He had started in a winter-cold Jerusalem, where the rain
fell unceasingly. The houses, which seemed to him to be no
more than caves carved into the old city's enormous rock
outcrops, breathed cold dampness, and he walked around
with wet feet regretting he had neglected to bring enough
changes of socks. He rambled dutifully around the alleyways,
anxious not to miss important historical monuments, as if
his journey was just another examination. Here he was
picked up by an elderly white-bearded Jew who introduced
himself as a Canadian and spoke with the same cheerful
drawl as the numerous young Americans who thronged the
city's youth hostel. In a crypt below the Church of the Holy
Sepulchre the Canadian asked for a kiss. Thomas, who felt
he owed a debt of gratitude because the old man had devoted
a couple of hours to him, kissed the white beard cautiously.
The old man grew bolder and began to describe his relationship with an Armenian priest, who each time they reached
their 'climax', a word whose exact meaning in this connec-
tion Thomas was slightly hazy about, had raised his eyes to
the ceiling and exclaimed: 'How wonderful are the works
of Our God,' a sentence the Canadian found absurd as he
couldn't see what God had to do with their relationship.
When he reached the end of his story and saw the expression

on Thomas's face he regretted his attempt at seduction. Instead he presented Thomas with two pairs of socks and instructed him on the importance of keeping his feet dry, after which he let him go.

Thomas had made for the east. It was winter. In the snow-covered mountains somewhere in eastern Turkey he had stood and stared at a bus that had broken down. The bus was parked at the edge of the road, its body covered with dirt, dried mud on the bumpers and wheels. It was hardly a vehicle, merely jumbled pieces of metal and glass the wind had blown together and brought to rest in the vicinity of each other. A note of silence came from the surrounding mountains, it was like a diktat.

He had thought about the incident. He often did. He was very inclined to see himself as blurred, as if his existence ran out into many words and symbols without ever completely filling them out. The words were too big for him, like clothes made for someone more fully grown. He had stood there in the mountains thinking he might as well have been born there as in any other place. And that it was only the electric spark in an engine that separated him from the frozen landscape. He looked at the blue snow fields higher up the ridge of the mountain that had been levelled out by millions of years' alternation between heat and cold. Further down were gleaming black slopes too steep for the snow to lie on, as if the mountains had sweated from the effort of carrying their own monstrous weight. Not far from the road stood one or two houses made of piled stones, mere protuberances in a landscape that emanated no more than a merciless emptiness his imagination would never be able to fill.

Later on a snowstorm took him by surprise. It was on the border between Iran and Afghanistan. The buses were held up for several days. The enforced confinement came almost as a relief to him. The flat landscape outside the hotel was filled with a dazzling glare when the huge snow-flakes threw back cascades of light from the sun. He lived on sugar and green tea, served in little enamelled metal teapots. He sat in a vestibule, the only room in the mud-walled building with windows. The uneven glass made the horizon take abrupt unmotivated leaps. He warmed his hands on his mug. He had emptied his rucksack and was wearing all his clothes as protection against the cold. He had put the spare socks given him by the Canadian Jew on top of his own. His boots had given way under the pressure until the seams burst and the uppers turned their noses in the air. When a snow plough eventually got through from the Afghan side he was overwhelmed by the monstrousness of his journey and visualized himself vanishing without trace in the snow. Soldiers with shovels on their shoulders had been called out, they ran beside the slowly advancing column of vehicles. An overloaded lorry capsized in a cloud of snow. For a moment he wished he had been in it and would not need to travel further.

After the snowstorm his body was drained of warmth. Cold rattled inside him, his clothes lay in stiff layers and scraped his skin. He crept out of his cocoon in a public bath in Herat. He felt like an insect whose carapace had split. But inside was still only a defenceless worm.

Again he had felt the terror. The scalding hot water gave him back warmth, but the steam and the fierce men's bodies around him had a suffocating effect. The men were

22

powerful and lean in unexpected places. Even their obesity spoke of aggression and hardness. The skin on their bearded faces was like thick leather and gathered in heavy folds and wrinkles above the root of the nose and down the cheeks. Their eyes were deep set, filled with a dark anger he could not interpret. He felt like a spy, but the sight of their naked bodies did not bring him closer to them. On the contrary, it was a dangerous moment. He was suddenly alarmed by the water and had to struggle not to hit out in panic.

Triumph over the many kilometres he had put behind him turned into the reverse. Water ran into his ears and throat. He felt totally immersed in foreignness, as if threatened with drowning and disappearance.

He had read that the Indians had come like an immigration of sculptors through the land. Each time they had encountered rock they had dug their way through it with hammer and chisel. So their temples were in caves or suddenly rose up in the midst of the sand, carved out of one single stone. That was how they had built their country, like the sculptor who creates a figure out of a block of stone by taking away and taking away and never for a moment adding anything.

They had created not only their temples but also their bodies in the same manner. Their bones were visible under the same polished skin, with the muscles like fragile threads, draped over a bared shoulder or a harmoniously formed chest, over them yet another drapery, the folds in a shawl loosely slung around the body. They stood clad in white in river beds with metre-long saris whose gauzy fabric was held up in the wind to dry, flying like flags, a calf slept on the pavement beneath the plaited rope base of a bed, a

23

human being stretched out on the bed in deep affinity with the animal, wrapped in the same cloth that at other times served as his clothes, and which he might even die in, his only ones, always these oxen in the picture, with white skins taut over their backs between big bones, this paradox of starvation that hunger tautens the skin as if it was too small for the shrivelling body, always with the same mildness, human and animal, the heavy heads of the oxen bowed towards the earth, the faces in the black shadow of turban or shawl, all following the same destiny, over the desert sand, through dried-out river beds, in streets that were not thoroughfares but landscapes of bodies, always in movement, with the same calm as the bird which lets itself be borne on a rising air current, without a wing beat.

It was as if with every step they took, every bending of the head, every shadow they cast on the earth, every hand that held a hungry child's body in a protective clasp, or created an ornament, forever changing but never breaking, merely transformed itself.

When he saw the Indians walk, then he would understand. Understand, that word which he cogitated over with all the thirst for knowledge he had in him, and which should preferably be without an object, for then it was most absolute. To understand, not the world, not himself, but to demolish this very distinction into limitless expansion, complete fusion. To create himself as the sculptor creates his sculptures, by taking away and taking away. Until he reached the most elementary part, the foot, which moves. That was his reason for coming to India: to see the Indians walk. To see their ash-grey feet moving over the silver-white dust. His imaginative faculty worked in the black and white scale of photography, he knew that very well but he was certain that those were the innermost colours of the country, because it was only black and white and the encounter between them that embodied calmness and purity. It was in ash grey and silver white that he would reach his understanding: to see a human being walk and not get any nearer his goal or distance himself from it, but instead walk with each step as a goal in itself in a constant creation and annihilation of all movement and direction.

That was how he had dreamed of it at home, books of photography in his hand, about a land where the rocks turned into lace, and life was like the folds the wind made in a flag, you didn't know whether the wind was in the flag or the flag in the wind, and it was both.

He was miles away. The dark restaurant with the small islands of light above the tables and the intimacy of another person made him sleepy. He nodded and came to with a start. The Indian was staring at him from across the table. He did not know how long he had been dreaming. He blinked, wanted to rub his face, but that would be too childish.

'My young friend,' the other said, 'I can see you are tired. You must rest. It is important, when you are faced with so many dramatic impressions. But before we part — allow me to make a suggestion. Let us travel a stretch together. Then I shall show you India.'

'How can you just go away? Haven't you any work to do? And your family?'

'I told you I travel a lot. It is my work. I am a writer. Travel articles. I feel sympathetic towards you. Let me be your friend. I can help you with the practical side of your journey, and — I assure you — you will not find a better guide. In return I may perhaps collect material for an article or two.'

He put out his hand and smiled, showing his teeth.

'Well, what do you say? Shall we be friends?'

3

The money-changers plied their trade in a narrow street off one of the main thoroughfares. Their agents swarmed all over the district and tried to start up negotiations with every passing foreigner.

'Change of money, sir?'

They jutted their heads forward and withdrew them next moment as if regretting it. Then they looked around them in conspiratorial fashion and discreetly beckoned the potential customer to go along with them.

There were so many of them that most were left doing nothing. They performed their pantomimes in the open air and kept up their secretive whispering patiently until someone stopped and allowed themselves to be led away. The turbans worn by most of them made their foreheads lower and their eyes sink even deeper in behind the thick black brows. There was an aura of mystery in the money-changers' district that made Thomas see the simple exchange of money on the black market as an alchemical process, only accessible to the initiated, inaccessible to him.

George kept a few steps ahead all the time. He allowed himself to be stopped several times. An agent would pull him into a doorway or behind a column. There followed a quick exchange of words, Thomas stood a couple of metres away unable to understand what was being said, only now and then a figure would be uttered in English. Their expressions looked as if they were making game of one another. They smiled provocatively at each other like a pair of lovers and then shot their eyebrows skywards in mutual contempt. The urge to swindle was written so clearly on the grimacing faces, they performed unceasing gymnastics with their various features so it looked like a show of knife-throwing or tightrope-walking with two virtuosi challenging each other.

The actual exchange of money was not carried on in the street. People allowed themselves to be led away by an agent whose attitude changed abruptly from ingratiation to indifference now his prey was hooked. He strutted briskly off ahead of them, they just had to follow him, now and then he stopped to exchange a word with a street trader while he threw a glance over his shoulder to make sure they were still with him.

To Thomas's astonishment, the centre for the black money market was equipped with official-looking placards covering the whole façade of a house and announcing exchange of money. The secretive huckstering vanished completely, they just walked in from the street with the agent. In the middle of a white-painted room an elderly man sat behind a desk. His massive body was enveloped in a loose shirt which coldly reflected a neon light on the ceiling. A few men squatted on their haunches along one wall with their arms resting on their knees. They gestured loosely with their hands while they talked.

The man at the desk stretched out his hand and asked Thomas for his passport. Behind him the group along the wall stopped their discussion and moved across to the desk, where they started to imitate the old man's movements. First they bent down to join in scrutinizing the passport, then they looked up from the photograph of Thomas as if on command and back again, satisfied with the comparison. The man slowly leafed through the passport. He studied every single stamp as if it held hidden information on the owner of the passport. Once he lifted it to his nose and sniffed at it. Then he asked Thomas to sign the travellers' cheques. He took hold of the first one and held it up to the light. Thomas followed his gaze and was almost blinded by the glare from the neon tube.

'This is not your signature!' roared the man suddenly.

Thomas gave a start.

'It is my signature.' He looked appealing at the massive figure on the chair behind the desk.

'But it is my signature,' he repeated without conviction.

George took him soothingly by the arm.

'Don't mind him,' he whispered, 'he's just a crazy man.'

He turned towards the desk. 'If you are not satisfied we can find another place for exchange. You are not the only one. Come, we'll be going.' He looked encouragingly at Thomas, at the same time winking the eye furthest from the desk.

The men in the room stared. Thomas thought they looked like animals.

'OK, I'll give the lad a chance.' The big man spoke to George as if it was a matter between the two of them. 'Tell him he must go on writing his name here until I say stop.'

He pushed a piece of paper across the table. Thomas looked at George, who nodded at the paper. He started to write. His hand shook and he could not write rhythmically. The letters fell on top of each other like a collapsing card house. Every time he wrote his name it grew worse. In the end it wasn't even a name, just random squiggles, silly variations, like those a child who had not learned to write would try to make into the outlines of proper lettering. The man let him go on. He gave up and threw down the ballpen.

'I can't do it.' He put his hands to his eyes.

'That's all right. I am satisfied. Sign your travel cheques.'

The man put his hand into a drawer and brought out an untidy bundle of notes held together by a rubber band and clip. He tossed the bundle over to Thomas almost disgustedly.

'Take care of the money. This is a dangerous district.'

'Very dangerous.'

The band behind him echoed with exaggerated stress on each syllable, as if they wanted to spell out something or other. Then they wagged their heads.

4

The windows were just small squares with bars over them.
They had no glass. The luggage rack was so low that he hit
his head on it when he stood up. George pushed his rucksack
into place. While they waited to start people kept on
streaming in. There were no walls separating the compart-
ments from the corridor through the carriage. This was
already chock full of people sitting down, their knees drawn
up under their chins to take up as little room as possible.
From the shelf above him feet dangled down to the height
of his forehead. Tea-sellers fought their way through with
kettles and a basket full of earthenware pots, calling their
shrill 'Chai, chai!' Others were selling bottles of mineral
water in various colours, green, yellow and red. When
the bottle was finished the customers struggled against the
stream in the packed carriage and held out their hands to
get their deposit returned. Women in faded saris offered
half-rotten bananas and coconuts. Others sold rice dishes
in a bowl of banana leaves fastened together with little
wooden sticks.

The screaming was overpowering. He heard the ferocity
in the voices, a dark fire burning down through the densely
packed train, it plucked the oxygen from his lungs.

Beggar boys pushed arms thin as sticks through the

small window bars trying to grab hold of the passengers, meanwhile kicking at the side of the train and making a drubbing sound all along its length. It sounded like an approaching thunderstorm. Now and then the urchin swarm was split up when a conductor or a porter in a red turban struck out at them. The next moment they were back clinging stubbornly to the windows.

Cripples crawled around begging. Their withered limbs, dragged along after them, resembled the legs of squashed insects. Minute bodies with hydrocephalic heads hobbled awkwardly between the seats like punctured balls gone astray, imploringly lifting their melancholy faces to the passengers. When they approached he drew in his legs and huddled into his corner.

There seemed to be no bursting point at which the stream of people would have to stop. He looked out at the platform where new crowds had already stationed themselves, waiting with bovine patience for the next train, whose arrival would immediately spark off a lethal struggle to reach the empty seats. A foot suddenly appeared at the window. Then two hands seized hold of the horizontal window bars and a body blocked the view. Several more followed. For a while the compartment was left almost in darkness, while one figure after another climbed up on to the roof.

As the train began to move there was a tremendous gust of heat from the locomotive just in front. The beggar boys let go of the windows and ran along beside the train yelling. Cripples and dropsical heads crawled down the steps head-first and let themselves drop the last bit. Lying on the platform gathering strength they looked like bundles of clothes deserted by their owners. The vendors continued their bawling unconcerned, only one or two jumped off, swinging the bulky empty tea kettles.

The doors were left open. A hot gust of wind stirred the women's saris. The white jasmine flowers in their shining black hair nodded dozily.

At the next station he stepped out on to the platform and joined a crowd gathered around an earthenware tub of water. The drinkers lifted up a scoopful of water. The water fell into their open mouths in a sunlit stream without touching their lips. When he tried to imitate them it splashed over his face. The crowd laughed and explained their technique to him, opening their mouths wide and taking big swallows that went straight down into their stomachs. His lips happened to touch the edge of the scoop. They shouted at him, suddenly excited. Alarmed, he tried again, but spilt water down his shirt.

Later in the day he felt ill. A lassitude came over him, it started in his thigh muscles and made his knees give way. There was a queue for the toilet, and he wasn't sure he could hold back. He dared not say anything to George. If he didn't talk about it surely it would pass off. He joined the queue, didn't have the courage to push forward, afraid that if he stopped concentrating for one moment disaster would follow.

The lavatory consisted of a hole in the floor and two small raised foot-rests. Round the edge of the sunk porcelain pan was dried excrement, fresh lumps of it were on the pedals. Even the lower part of the walls was covered with it. His stomach turned over, but the place had him in its clutches. He tried not to breathe when he squatted, pulling down his trousers. The lurching of the train threatened to throw him to the fouled floor at any moment.

The heels of his boots were covered when he was finally able to relax his concentration and let go. It poured out of him in a hot uncontrollable stream that splashed his buttocks. There was no toilet paper, only a tap at floor level. With an effort that brought tears of self-pity to his eyes he had to put his hand between his buttocks and touch the greasy excrement. When he looked at his filthy hand, the smeared walls and the floor that was uneven with trodden black-brown shit seemed to close in around him.

He gasped for the air he had tried to keep out for so long, and the stench struck him with full force like a concentrate of the secretion from millions of nauseous bodies, a fetid gust from a disease that had raged for centuries.

He went back to his seat. The small windows with their bars gave him the feeling of moving from one enclosed space to another. He had rinsed his hand under the tap but not dried it. His fingers dripped, he held them out like a fan, as if to keep them from contact with each other. He huddled into his corner beside George again.

The heat pushed in through the window and laid a heavy hand over his mouth. His brain buzzed aggressively like a bee fallen on its back on a window sill.

The woman opposite caught his eye. She sat with her legs pulled up under her, half squatting in the confined space. On each of her feet were six toes. He stared again and counted. There were six toes. They lay there in a demure row, small and delicate, even the big toe scarcely differentiated, as if it was bashful about its special position,

34

and, conscious of the crush around it, forbade itself any individuality.

The brown feet filled him with the same disgust as the excrement in the toilet. He recalled the insect limbs of the cripples and the heavy swollen heads and felt that here, deformity was the rule. The floodwave of human beings that had engulfed the train and rose alongside it at each station pushed all natural laws aside and instead produced a fluid chaos in which life assumed haphazard forms. It was a wild growth, a kind of permanent birth pang traversing the human masses, related to the pains that wrenched his stomach with diarrhoea, an evacuation like a thought that knew no limits.

He slept restlessly that night. Every so often he woke and looked round at the sleepers in the dim light from a night bulb. Their bodies were shaken about unresistingly by the movements of the train like jellyfish slung about by the waves. They lay all over each other as if the limbs did not belong to anyone, they had taken them off as they fell asleep. In the morning they would collect them up again and take on the likeness of human beings, in sleep they melted together into a formless creature in which every individual characteristic was cancelled out.

With the coming of first light, briefly announced by a reddening in the sky, there was a moment's coolness. Life returned to the slumped bodies and they rose. One old man came to a halt and remained with his elbows on his knees while looking thoughtfully down at the floor. Their white shirts and loose trousers made them look as if they always wore night clothes. The relaxation of the night, an instinctive pleasure in the cessation of movement, still lurked beneath

35

the skin and emerged whenever they sat down for a moment or flopped with a hand beneath the head on the comfortless wooden benches of the compartment.

Most were thin, but those who were plumper had an air of harmony in their fatness, like that of a slowly ripened fruit. They were so unaccustomed to the movements of the day that they had to start themselves up like machines rusted up by long disuse. They rubbed their faces vigorously while pushing fingers into ears and mouths. They spat on the floor to supplement their visit to the toilet and make sure both ends were emptied. Between spits they hawked at length. In the course of the night their unused voices had gathered waste products of unpleasant sounds that had to be evacuated.

A man stuck his tongue out and scraped the deposit on it with a length of thread. Then he studied the thread carefully before cleaning it with two fingers.

At the first stop after sunrise the passengers crowded out of the train. They stood on the platform in long rows gargling with a fearful sound. Thomas stayed in his seat by the window. George went out on to the platform with the crowd but contented himself with splashing his face with water.

Thomas was grateful to him for what he regarded as a moment of normal behaviour.

George brought back a little earthenware jar of tea. The tea was without milk and spices, and Thomas drank it obediently. He said no to two bananas, they were soft with black spots.

George sat down opposite him. 'Your first Indian diarrhoea,' he said, 'and it will not be your last. But one day your stomach will have settled down. The flora in the gut changes. Maybe before you do, if you understand what I mean.'

He laughed in a way Thomas found hurtful.

'Thomas, Thomas, don't look so offended. Do you think I didn't see your face when you came back from the toilet? It's worse for your face than your stomach. And believe me, I know. You see, in my parents' house there were two bathrooms. In one there was a lavatory like those you have at home, a porcelain pan with a seat you can put up and down, which is meant to sit on. In the other bathroom there was a lavatory too. And that consisted of a porcelain pan, only it didn't have a seat, but two foot pedals, one on each side, exactly like the toilet on the train here, where the pedals are just put one on each side of a hole in the floor. The toilet was a true compromise between East and West. My parents had two toilets to show that they were certainly good patriotic Indians, but at the same time they were modern people who kept up with the times. The semi-Oriental model was intended for our relatives from the country. They crawled up on to the edge and squatted there high up while shitting down in the pan or all over the place, as is the habit of us Indians. You know that squatting position. You must have seen my countrymen sitting for hours in the shade of a tree or a wall. Maybe you ask yourself how they can stand it, but they can, they have found a balancing point when they sit with their behind rocking a score of centimetres above the ground and their outstretched arms resting on their sharp kneecaps. That position is just as natural to us as lying down.'

He peeled one of the bananas. 'Nobody used the other

toilet in my parents' house, the European one. No one, that is, except me. It was because of my urge to explore, my curiosity, I always wanted to try something new. You Europeans sit upright when you shit, don't you, you're always alert, so I grew to be like that too.'

He studied the peeled banana before taking a bite. When he had chewed it he went on: 'That's why I'm sitting in this train today, always on the lookout for new adventures. You could say that my un-Indian future was decided on a toilet seat.'

He laughed, obviously pleased with himself. Thomas managed a chuckle too.

5

Well into the morning, when the heat was already at culmi-
nation point, they left the train. Thomas staggered when he
walked into the sun. Impressions hit him like blows. He ran
for the shade below a lean-to roof, he just wanted to stand
there with his eyes closed. George seized him by the arm
and led him through the wall of shouting porters. They
were soon out in the street, where the cycle rickshaws were
besieging the station. The wallahs rang their bells aggressively when Thomas came in sight.

'Where are we?'

George uttered a name Thomas could not catch in the
din. 'We'll stay here for a day or two.'

The houses had balconies with frail railings. Behind
these, doors were cut into the walls, the balconies clung to
the buildings like birds' nests on a mountainside. People
swarmed everywhere, but they did not look as if they
belonged to the houses or in fact would be able to go in or
out of the small door openings. They looked like adults
imprisoned in dolls' houses. The railings around the balconies reached no higher than their knees, they had to lower
their heads when they went through the doors. There was
a constant dizzying alternation between proportions. The
openings in the houses seemed too small for the people

moving in and out, and the houses themselves far too big, like eroded mountains with their crumbling whitewash and damp-spotted walls. Electric cables hung in twisted bundles among the houses like a wild, random growth of liana and parasitic plants. It was like passing through some deserted civilization, a town rediscovered in the jungle after centuries of decay and neglect, and discovering a populace still inhabiting the ruins, aimlessly wandering around, hypnotized by the mysterious power of the past, with no recollection of whether they themselves had created these buildings or merely found them.

They drove past a row of shops like little cubes open to the street. In the middle of them white-clad men sat on cushions surrounded by wares. One of them caught Thomas's eye, for an instant they looked into each other's eyes, the other sat unmoving. His white tunic shone out, his face was one with the half-darkness, only the eyes caught a reflexion of the light outside. He looked like a secretion from the space around him, a human stalagmite that had dripped down from the ceiling, one with his situation on the cushion to such an extent that he seemed somewhere midway between an organic and an inorganic form of life. Thomas felt that his own steps, his heartbeat, the speed with which he moved through life, could be reckoned in seconds and minutes, theirs, the inhabitants of these houses, on the other hand, in centuries. So different were they from each other, they and he. For a second a glance had lit on him and it was as if someone had stared at ultraviolet light, and he was the ultraviolet in this person's eye, with a heart that vibrated at an incomprehensibly rapid frequency.

The sun blazed down. He crouched beside George in

the shadow beneath the little hood of the rickshaw. The wallah on the saddle in front of them bent over as he worked the heavy cycle. His calf sinews tautened as he half stood up to force the pedals round. His spine protruded like a knotty branch under the skin that shone with sweat. He had a cloth over his shoulder with which he impatiently wiped his bare chest. He made slow progress. His body twisted painfully at each push on the pedals. Now and then the wallah uttered a hollow cry, either in anger or reproach, the painful muscular effort had reached his vocal cords and stretched them to breaking point in a protest with which the whole of his agonized body resounded.

George slapped the bony back with the flat of his hand. 'Quicker!'

Thomas stared in horror. He expected a furious outburst. Instead the skinny body leaned over the handlebars as if to show eagerness. George turned to Thomas with a smile.

'He must work for his money.'

They stopped in front of a whitewashed house. Steps led up to large double doors from which remains of blue paint flaked from the furrowed grey wood. A huddled figure slept, half covered by a dirty yellow garment, in the strip of shadow along the house wall. A skinny rump stuck out in the sun.

The pavement was covered with ashes. Under a piece of sackcloth could be seen the black burned base of a tin cooking pot. Beside it a water-buffalo stood chewing the cud. Its big horns were twisted like spiral snail shells. Their tips had been sawn off a few centimetres from its broad skull, as if at the last moment some merciful soul had

41

wanted to prevent the horns from piercing the buffalo's brain. George patted the animal on the head as they walked past and grinned at Thomas. The buffalo went on chewing unconcerned, ignorant of the deception nature had practised on it. Its damp muzzle shone black in the sunshine.

George pushed the door open and led Thomas into a big room that had once been white but was now grey with dust. At the far end a door led out into a yard. In the middle of the yard was a lead-lined water tank, on its edge stood a row of small brass pots. A fat man was pouring water over himself from one of the pots. His stomach shone wetly and he slapped it merrily when he caught sight of George.

They exchanged greetings by putting the tips of their fingers together and raising their hands to their foreheads. At the same time they bowed slightly towards each other. To Thomas they seemed to smile ironically.

George told Thomas to give the man a banknote.

'This is our host. He loves sweet things.'

The fat man rolled his head affirmatively and rubbed his distended stomach as if to emphasize that it was tyrannically responsible for his sweet tooth.

In one corner of the yard Thomas caught sight of a small statue. It was of a dancing woman with a narrow waist and broad hips. The body of the statue was draped in a white cloth, it gave the figure a light, almost swaying movement. The breasts, which were strong and rounded, were high. The hands were long and slim, one had the index and little fingers pointing upwards, the other was bent at the wrist while thumb and little finger met and touched lightly. The whole body swayed gracefully and the impression of

42

playful abandonment would have been complete if it had not been for the symmetrical face, in which a curved nose and two crossed eyes gathered themselves into an expression of formidable willpower and concentration, as if the dancer was not so much abandoned as imperious, demanding veneration and worship.

The fat man had followed Thomas's glance. He went over to the statue and turned towards Thomas.

'You do not understand,' he said in broken English. 'You think – woman?'

He looked at Thomas enquiringly.

Thomas nodded, uncomprehending. 'Yes, woman.'

The fat man started to laugh, the whole of his body shook.

'No – not woman.'

He whisked the white cloth off the statue. Between the wide hips hung a massive penis. The bronze shone with wear, as if the organ was frequently touched.

'You see. Not woman. Man.' He laughed again.

George laughed as well.

The fat man pointed to the statue's breasts. 'No. Not man – woman.'

Thomas stood rigid with aversion. They were making fun of him by a secret agreement they had come to from the moment George and the fat man had bowed to each other.

George noticed his unease and stopped laughing.

'The statue represents wholeness,' he said placatingly. 'Both sexes in one person. It is religious symbolism.'

Thomas made no reply. It ought to represent deception, he thought. Its meaning is concealed with a cloth, after all.

Their apartment was a high-ceilinged rectangular room

which made Thomas think of a crevice in a rock. A small peephole at the far end threw a dusty slanting shaft of light down a bare stone wall. Two mattresses lay crosswise on the floor. The room was so narrow that both ends touched the bare stone walls.

He threw himself down on the stained cover. It was a relief to close his eyes. He drew the darkness around him and curled himself into a ball.

'Is the boy sick?' he heard the fat man ask.

Some time later George woke him up. He squatted in front of the mattress holding out a glass of tea for Thomas. He had brought two bananas as well. They were yellow all over and had no blemishes. Thomas ate them. His stomach contracted. He didn't know if it was from hunger or his innards sinking into a vortex like the water running down the drain in a bath.

'Let us go for a walk. It will do you good.'

Thomas got to his feet unwillingly. He was ill. Ill people should lie down. He could feel an immense longing for cool rooms coming over him, starched sheets, the scent of cleanliness. But the diarrhoea had drained him of will. He drooped, put his hand to his forehead.

'Come along now!'

George was impatient. Thomas followed him in a daze.

In the yard he avoided looking at the statue.

The prone figure outside the house had gone, but the cooking pot still lay in the ashes. The water-buffalo went on chewing, unconcerned at wearing on its head the question mark nature had imposed on its large blood-filled body. A girl squatted broodingly beside the tin cooking pot, her matted hair hung down hiding her face, only one naked shoulder stuck out from the mass of hair.

The street was just as full of people as earlier in the day. The sight of this swarming humanity made Thomas think that life in the Indian streets never rested. He pictured the streets running continuously from town to town like veins, sometimes stretching just under the skin, sometimes diving down into the mysteries of the flesh, always filled with people sitting and walking, everywhere those bloodshot eyes with their yellowish glow, everywhere the same bony foreheads glistening beneath the hammer blows of the sun.

Here in the Indian street he had to go with the stream, here he had no choice. If he lost the rhythm for a moment a cycle mudguard immediately scraped his leg, or a hand came down on his shoulder in warning. Only the cows crossed the stream, tossing their heads as if permanently irritated by the swarming flies. He had to watch his step, each movement demanded his attention, he was used to another kind of traffic's stuttering rhythm, here everything moved like a huge body, people and animals, eyes and skin.

A group of women came dancing towards him. They had slung one end of their scarlet saris around their heads, an interwoven pattern of gold thread wriggled in the white sunlight like a covering of living snakes, coins dangled before their painted eyes, the caste marks were fiery yellow, they all had beauty spots in the same place on their cheeks. Their arms swayed to and fro over their heads like cobras worked into a state of excitement by the music of a shrill flute, gold bangles rattled on their arms. Several wore flared skirts that flew out around them while they danced round and round. They whirled past, sweat assailed his nostrils, he saw dark patches under the upstretched arms, the cloth around them was faded with white salty edges. One of the dancers stroked his cheek with a long painted nail, a pair of eyes looked deep into his, she opened her mouth and let her tongue play towards him. He drew back and collided with someone behind him.

Then the women were gone. The crowd had not made way for them, it rather seemed as if they had gone through a wall without meeting any resistance.

Drums beat nearby, a fresh group appeared. These were men dressed in red, they had white bandages on their hands, held the drumsticks awkwardly, the blows had no strength in them.

'They are lepers,' he heard George say. 'Try and look at their faces.'

Thomas averted his eyes after glimpsing pink excoriations in the almost black skin. When he found the courage to look up again the drummers had already passed.

Further on they came upon more lepers. It was near a river, the street opened up, Thomas breathed in the air with relief, at the end of the street lay the river, reflecting the sky that was white in the afternoon heat, the opposite bank writhed like a flickering mirage, it was a flat pink sandy shore, perhaps the beginning of a desert. Beside some steps which led down to the water the lepers were unwinding bandages of dirty rags from their wasted limbs. At first he saw only the same pinkish abraded skin as before, almost like a mutation in the dark pigmentation, then he caught sight of stumps of hands with no fingers and doll-like club feet from which the whole row of toes had gone. The noseless faces nodded and writhed in the grimaces the lepers used to express their misery. Their bodies were black as asphalt as if they had lived close to a fire that had gradually scorched them and burned away the extremities of their

46

limbs. Nature had regretted her work of creation and was taking back what she had given, not at one swoop, but piece by piece.

In the heat that was affecting his vision he seemed to see the outlines of the lost hands and feet flickering around the stumps.

A fire was burning at the foot of the steps. The eager leaping of the flames towards a vanishing point a couple of metres in the air was the only movement on the deserted river bank. Behind it the water was calm, as if the river had coagulated in the heat. A white cloth in the pyre caught fire, clumps of ash immediately shot up. A brown scorched foot with its ankle swollen emerged from the flames. A human being was burning up in there. The foot slowly bent, as if the burning body stretched itself. The leg grew longer and at the same time slimmer. Then the foot fell down with a gliding movement.

It was like watching a candle melting.

6

'Are you married?'

Thomas couldn't help laughing.

'You laugh? Do you find the question so absurd?'

Thomas shook his head and smiled placatingly.

'Have you tried going with an Indian woman?' George persevered.

'I didn't think you could.'

'Of course you can.'

'I thought you had to be married.'

'You do. I'm talking of prostitutes.'

'I'd never dream of paying for a woman.'

'You don't need to, surely. Where you come from a man can do as he likes, can't he?'

George laughed ironically. He took a slurp from the whisky bottle and dried his mouth with the back of his hand. Then he leaned his head back and closed his eyes. His face shone wet in the hard light from an unshaded bulb on the ceiling.

It had grown hotter. They had been travelling south all the time. Luckily the hotel room was better than the first one. They slept on real beds even if the sheets were grey and full of holes. They couldn't be spending much money. He left the bills to George, who asked for a note or two now and again. Then Thomas took out the shapeless bundle with its rubber band and paper clip, but it didn't seem to him to get much smaller. He didn't eat much. Bananas and a small portion of rice, but he didn't like the gritty feel of the grains against his throat. At least his reduced appetite spared him the horror of visiting the toilet. Now days could go by in between.

George opened his eyes again. A quiver ran through his lower lip.

'Now tell me honestly, my dear foreign friend, what do you really think of Indian women?'

For a moment his lower lip looked as if it would drop off, then it stretched in an encouraging smile.

In New Delhi Thomas had seen beautiful Indian women strolling arm in arm with their saris flung over their shoulders and their soft midriffs revealed. He had fantasized about their heavy shining hair that could cover him up and enclose him like a tent. But there he stopped. He couldn't speak their language, not even that between men and women.

'The Indian women are beautiful,' he replied. 'Like butterflies. It is a different culture. I don't know what else to say.'

In the afternoon they had sat in a coffee house and stared down at the street as a wedding procession passed by. The low-ceilinged place, which was on the first floor, had the same mysterious intimacy as a cave in a treetop. The walls were covered with carved panels, and narrow benches were placed beside minute tables, which grew out of the shiny worn planks of the floor like wide-capped mushrooms.

Down in the street a group of musicians shrilled atonally on instruments somewhat like trumpets. Some men twirled around holding up big silvery lamps. At the back of the procession a boy sat unmoving on a white horse, under his turban his face was both childish and melancholy, the golden skin shone with oil and gave him the appearance of a lacquered statue. It was the bridegroom. He looked like a prisoner of war being led through the streets to sacrifice.

George took another drink. He looked at Thomas teasingly.

'Ah, my Thomas. Why am I drinking, then? I can see it makes you unhappy. You draw back from me. You don't trust me when I'm drunk.'

He put down the whisky bottle on the mattress and stretched his legs out in front of him. The sudden alteration in weight tipped the bottle over. With a swift movement he caught it in its fall. The bottle, still three-quarters full, spurted out over the sheet. It made a dark stripe on the grey cloth.

He dried it with his hand. Then he turned his gaze back to Thomas.

'Shall I tell you a secret?'

He made a pause for effect. Thomas did not reply.

'Don't you want to hear it? Well, I'll tell you anyway. I am the best whisky drinker in India. That is my secret.'

He held out the bottle of whisky and made the dark brown glass flash in the light from the bulb in the ceiling. 'The best,' he repeated. He sat in silence for a while, as if he wanted to give Thomas time to digest the information. Then he went on:

'Have you ever seen a bunch of Indian businessmen

getting drunk? No, of course you haven't. But you should. It's really an amazing sight. They meet at sundown when they have shut up shop. Then they sit in a back room and toast each other. They take mouthfuls so big.'

He measured with thumb and finger.

'In a short while they're half seas over. Their heads droop and when they think no one is looking they grimace. You see, they hate the taste of whisky. They would much prefer to eat sweet things, just like children. Have you tried whisky?'

He held out the bottle to Thomas. Thomas drew back.

'No, thanks, I don't feel like it.'

'You're wiser than my countrymen. Shall I tell you what whisky tastes of? You lose the desire to talk to others when you drink it. You even start to stop dreaming. Instead you see yourself. That's what there is in the bottle: loneliness. That's what makes me the best whisky drinker in India. The others don't know how to appreciate the taste. But I do.'

George stood up and edged along between the beds. He started to rummage in his suitcase.

'Now to work. We mustn't forget the object of our journey.'

He pulled out a pile of crumpled papers.

'I'll read you something.'

He threw Thomas a meaning glance. Then he buried his nose in the papers and leafed through them.

'Let's see. Where is it? I always forget to date my daily notes. All these temples! Haven't we had enough of temples soon, Thomas?'

He started to read aloud.

'Today we visited the temple at T. In the middle of the

courtyard stands a large black ox, carved out of a single block of stone. The stone weighs twenty-six tons and the ox is the second largest sculpture of its kind in India. We read these details in a leaflet we bought at a little office beside the entrance to the temple. The ox lies on a slope with its legs drawn up under it. There is a roof over it which gives it constant shade. Its position a metre or two higher than the surface of the courtyard and the half darkness under the roof makes the impression of its size all the more overwhelming. Now and again a white muslin cloth hanging from its massive shoulders stirs in the breeze. Then the ox seems almost alive, as if the immobility of the great body is not due to the stone but was some huge creature's own philosophical calm.

'We went up the steps to touch it. The surface of the stone was as smooth as human skin and almost as warm. Even though the ox is in the shade it still manages to absorb some of the sun's heat.

'Sitting beside the ox Thomas read aloud from the leaflet, which tells that according to a legend the sculpture was originally much smaller. But it suddenly began to grow until it reached its present size. All the signs were that it would have gone on growing if they had not driven an iron spike into its back. Inside the stone was a live frog and it was that which was responsible for the ox's growth. The frog was removed and put into a nearby pond. The leaflet adds reassuringly that this story is only based on rumours and hardly on reality. Thomas found this very amusing.'

George paused and took yet another gulp of whisky. Then he went on reading.

'The temple courtyard is completely dominated by the

enormous tower in the centre. But the closer you get to the tower the more the structure seems to dissolve before your eyes. The temple tower actually consists of images of towers, a conglomeration of miniature buildings one on top of the other, just as flight after flight of steps succeed each other in a pyramid. Some of the miniature buildings are exact replicas of the mother tower. Everywhere are minute windows and doorways, or rather images of windows and doorways, that do not lead anywhere. They cannot be said to be walled up because there are no rooms behind them. All these sham openings are guarded by statues of gods that seem to have been placed there only to emphasize the inaccessibility of the whole edifice. Thus, rather than an edifice, that tower is a monument to an edifice, a gigantic sculpture constructed of an almost infinite number of reproductions of itself.

'It is not a temple that invites its believers inside. It is true that on the bottom floor of the tower there are two small rooms in which temple ceremonies are held. Here a half-naked priest with painted torso swings a censer before the image of a god which is black and greasy from the smoke of the oil lamps and lumps of butter smeared on it as sacrifices. But the small sooty rooms, hardly more than three metres high, merely seem to emphasize the self-sufficiency of the enormous mass of stone that rears above them. Here rules a pantheon that has refused admittance to its worshippers. All that is left is the endlessly self-repeating form of faith, any substance was long since blocked up in petrified inaccessibility.

'On the third storey of the temple tower stands a row of historical figures. One of them is a European wearing a bowler hat. Our leaflet explains that there is much disagreement as to who the figure represents. Some maintain it is Marco Polo and see his presence as excellent proof of the cosmopolitan views of Indian culture. Others think it is an Englishman and that the sculptor's source of inspiration was an astrologer who foretold the approaching conquest of our country. The sculpture was erected several centuries before the English came to India.

'I asked Thomas which hypothesis he preferred. He replied that he liked the last one best. It was an attractive idea, that an edifice could display the image of the enemy that would one day come to crush the building's creators.

'We walked around the tower with our heads leaning back several times but did not succeed in finding the Englishman.'

George put down his bundle of papers. His face collapsed now that the effort demanded by the reading was over. Then he pointed a wavering finger at Thomas.

'You, you, you,' he repeated several times. 'You don't know what loneliness is.'

His finger went on pointing at Thomas as if he had forgotten it.

'Do you know how many gods we Indians have? Three hundred and thirty-three million. It's true. I'm not telling a lie.'

He wagged his head energetically as if to ward off any objection Thomas might have. The finger went on pointing.

'Three hundred and thirty-three million. Do you know how many Hindus there are? Four or five hundred millions. How long have there been so many of us? Ten years, twenty at most. That means that in three thousand or so years of

Hinduism the religion has had more gods than adherents. Isn't that a comical thought?'

His head fell forward and he chuckled into his chest. He must have spilt his whisky, there were patches on his shirt. His finger made circles and pointed at the ceiling for a moment as if he was accusing the overflowing heavens.

'Three hundred and thirty-three million gods. More gods than believers. More gods than our thinking has concepts for. More gods than there are words in the language. How then can you even talk about them? Have you a god, Thomas? Think about it. What does he do for you? He unifies your world, doesn't he? He gives you some words that are more important than all the others, goodness, righteousness, love, isn't that a word you use constantly in your world? Your god gives you a meaning. He selects the words for you and shows you that some words are more important than others. But my three hundred and thirty-three million gods? There are thousands of them for every word I know. They are like a mortar. They pulverize the words into small particles, they do not give me a meaning for life, they give me countless meanings that are so small that it's hardly possible to think them. When I look at my gods I feel I need a microscope. But how do I find such a microscope, Thomas? You in the West have discovered that everything is composed of molecules. A horse consists of molecules. A table consists of molecules. It's the same with our gods. They are a kind of molecule in our thought. They can be found in every single word. Maybe they are just electrical oscillations in our language. That kind of thing makes me dizzy, Thomas.'

His outstretched finger trembled in Thomas's direction

again. Thomas stared at it fascinated as if the finger was an antenna that sent and received signals from space and was the actual organ with which George communicated with the world.

In the end the arm was pulled down by its own weight. George swayed forwards perilously. He was about to fall over the edge of the bed. Then he straightened himself with a jerk and sat upright for a moment with closed eyes before collapsing on to his side. The brown whisky bottle keeled over spilling the remains of its contents into the mattress.

Thomas picked up the bottle and put it on the floor.

7

The next evening George again sat facing Thomas.

'I want to tell you about my first love affair,' he said.

'I wasn't very old. It was my mother's sister. You needn't be surprised. Such things occur in Indian families more often than you might think. She wasn't what I'd call particularly beautiful. Of course she couldn't hide the fact that she was no longer young. But her skin was white, whiter than yours and without wrinkles. And her hair was finer than our hair normally is. She used a lot of powder to enhance her paleness, and when I think of her it's the soft feel of powder that I remember. I never saw her naked. She uncovered her shoulders for me and her breasts. But I never saw her lower body, though she helped me up through the numerous layers of her sari. She had always taken care to powder those parts of her body she did show me. The powder lay on her shoulders and breasts and surrounded her body with a slightly downy aura. Only her nipples were unpowdered. They were large and very dark.'

He fell silent a moment as if to keep hold of the image.

'She always went round in a pair of big ugly horn-rimmed glasses. Behind them her face was delicate and narrow. In a strange way the glasses gave the impression of something girlish and untouched in her face, for they showed that in a very innocent way she didn't care if she was attractive to men or not. Sometimes when I was in bed with her she kept her glasses on. I thought it showed extreme passion when she closed her eyes behind the glass of her spectacles. I think I felt flattered too. I fancied she kept her glasses on because she wanted to see my body as clearly as possible. I didn't think she made me a man by taking me to bed with her. On the contrary, I was quite sure that it was just my underdeveloped boy's body that attracted her. It made me feel secure. There wasn't anything I had to live up to when I was with her. I could be myself. Or rather, I could accept my own incompleteness. There isn't really any story to tell. It began and it stopped again as such things usually do. She was alone a lot. Her husband was a merchant and away the whole time. He didn't love her. I was alone too, in the way you are when you are young and your body suddenly starts to change. We cried a lot together. I think she cried for her vanished youth and her lack of freedom. Perhaps she also cried because otherwise she would have felt it was cynical to go to bed with her nephew. Instead she was forced to make the affair into something tragic and romantic. I cried when she cried, out of sympathy for her and for the body she never dared show me. Perhaps too out of powerlessness. And many other causes I did not myself understand.'

George stopped. He leaned his head on one hand and stared in front of him, pondering. His elbow rested on his knee. He sat like that for a while. Then he turned to Thomas.

'You don't really like eating, do you?'

'No, not really.'

'You don't care for the Indian curries?'

'No.'

'Nor for masala dosa either?'

'No, I don't.'

'Not even tandoori chicken?'

They smiled at each other. It was like a guessing game with questions and answers.

'What do they eat in your country?'

Thomas described rye bread and potatoes, liver paté and salami and cheese, and while he launched into details of the phenomenon of a fricadeller, he felt that in the company of the Indian he was about to solve a mystery.

'I had a food phobia as a child,' he said.

He was slowly filled with an urge to confide. His childhood came back to him. As he talked about food his jaws shaped themselves into an imitation of the chewing movements of his infant self. He demonstrated how he had been unable to swallow when his mouth had been filled with food. An incomprehensible weight immediately fell upon him and forced his face down through the years, down to the plate that still existed at the bottom of his memory, swimming in a brown sauce like the blood from a congealed wound.

The words continued to come. He couldn't stop now. The disclosure turned into a burden that was nourished and grew through its own fulfilment. An insatiable desire to be heard swelled in him.

He enlarged his description of the table he had sat at. In his recollection it grew into a landscape every bit as endless as the time he spent at the table. He could remember everything. The table was spread with yellowish greasy oilcloth with a pattern of wreathed roses. Cutlery flanked the plate. He had begun with a pusher when he was very small. It was silver rusted and yellowed with use. A name was engraved on the handle, Elise. She was a girl from his mother's family who had died many years before. Later on he was allowed to eat with a knife and fork. The knife had a brown bone handle. Its blunt edge made a loud clang against the edge of the plate. He could still recall the sound.

Then he came to his mother. She was always a source of guilt-feeling in him. He felt he was wicked when he refused to eat, and that his wickedness affected his mother. He often wished his mother was wicked so that her wickedness could join with his and he would be free from blame. But she suffered with him when she saw the agonies food caused him. She told him how she too had been tortured by food in childhood. She lost her figure and put on one that did not belong to her because she had too much food, and ever since, all her life she had had to struggle to dig it up again, from behind the layers of flesh and fat, the original figure that belonged to her and that was nice and made her able to like herself. Now she didn't care for herself and never would before she rediscovered the figure hidden within her. She told him about the Sunday dinners of her childhood, when the joints were so fatty that if the table was jolted they stood trembling on their dishes for half an hour, so huge and elastic were the collars of fat that enveloped them and which she had to take in and carry around until the day when her real figure managed to fight its way through. At that time he had thought that was what life looked like. The jolting of the table was like birth. Then the human being lay there on its plate and quivered in its fat for half an hour

60

until its trembling stopped and it was quiet again in what the grown-ups called death. His mother had another concept of death. She told him that if he did not eat he would fade away. That was something you said about plants that did not get enough water.

While he described his mother he involuntarily imitated her. His body shrank and his shoulders drooped until he turned into an elderly woman sitting on a chair grieving over her life.

George looked at him attentively. 'My affair with my mother's sister,' he said. 'Of course now I can see that she was a replacement for my mother, as I must have been a substitute for her grown son. We made our own little theatre together. We both had something we were in the course of losing but didn't want to let go of.'

He went on looking at Thomas. 'Have you heard about Ganesha, the elephant god?'

Thomas woke as if out of a doze. 'The fat man with the elephant head?'

'Yes, that's right. Do you know how he got his head?'

Thomas looked at him in bewilderment.

'His mother gave birth to him fully grown, while his father was away from home. When the father came home he found what he thought was a strange man in his wife's arms. He was so furious that he chopped off the stranger's head without realizing it was his own son. When he found out his mistake and could not bear having a son without a head, he gave him one from an elephant instead.'

George continued. 'In your world too there is a famous story about a son and a mother who desire each other. Both are punished. She hangs herself and he puts out his own

61

eyes. The story of the elephant god is an immoral story by comparison. Ganesha is punished and yet he doesn't do it properly. Does he learn anything from his experience? Perhaps he does, perhaps he doesn't. He becomes someone else and yet he doesn't. He still has his body. But a new head. It's a strange sort of spiritual mathematics. To be one and yet another. One plus another. Do you know what he is god of, Ganesha? He is the god of obstacles. It's him you pray to when you are faced with a demanding enterprise.'

'I was not born fully grown. And my mother died when I was quite small.' Thomas's voice was suddenly sharp.

'Forgive me, Thomas. I didn't know your mother was dead.'

George leaned forward and put his hand on Thomas's knee. It was the first time they had touched each other.

'My dear,' he said. He kept his hand there. It felt warm and dry on the bare knee.

'How old were you when your mother died?'

'I was six.' Thomas regained his normal voice and felt the need to confide in return. 'It's strange. I have a very clear recollection of her death, but I know it doesn't fit. She died in hospital. I stand in the doorway watching a doctor performing a post-mortem on her. My mother lies on her back with her arms at her sides. One arm has been skinned downwards, so muscles and sinews are revealed. The doctor pulls a muscle with pincers and causes her hand to move, as if she was still alive. With his free hand he makes the same movement as if demonstrating an anatomical principle to an invisible gathering of spectators. There, you see. I remember every single detail.'

The Indian stared at him intensely.

'How did you react?'

'I didn't react at all. It is a picture my imagination has created. I just don't know where it comes from. But when I see my mother with the doctor bending over her, it is as if I am strangely free from sorrow at her death. It often came to me as a child. Some children believe the dead go to heaven and picture them sitting on clouds. I pictured my mother having an autopsy, although I didn't even know what that meant.'

'Tell me about your country.'

And again Thomas became the child who had once stared across a table, through a window and out over the low damp land where earth and clouds held each other fast and made a mirror for each other.

At that time the earth was grey and flat like the underside of the clouds. Now and then it rained. The earth could rain too, but upwards, with plants that stretched towards the underside of the clouds. There were blue-grey types of grain which turned into bread. There was a kind of grass with long cutting stalks which grew in sand. When the wind blew through it the stalks turned upwards with a metallic flash as from a drawn sword. There were trunks with moss on them. And evergreen trees in a dark forest. They crushed each other, the clouds and the earth.

'And the sky,' asked George, 'where was the sky?'

'The sky,' replied Thomas, 'the sky was only a space between.'

8

In the narrow street he had to make way for an ox pushing its way through the crowd. It had a hump on its back that was bent over as if the burden of flesh had been too heavy. The collapsed hump rocked slowly to and fro with each step. The horns were bound round with dirty cloths. Their dangerous points stuck up, remains of red paint looked like a forgotten warning. Over the distended belly were impressions of hands in blue.

In front of them the street was blocked by a massive mountain of bricks, blackening as the vault of the sky darkened. Higher up two gilded spires caught the remains of the sunset. They ascended a flight of stone steps. From the topmost step they could look out over the town, whose flat roofs were swiftly fading from sight in the mellow dark red of the tropical dusk. Through a gateway they entered a square full of seated people in white tunics. A flock of crows disappeared into the darkness with flapping wings.

George took off his shoes and made a sign to Thomas. The stones were warm to the feet. They still held the heat of the sun. None of the white-clad figures stared as they walked towards one of the slim towers.

A narrow spiral staircase led up into total darkness. Now and again through small windows at floor level came

64

a faint light that allowed him to glimpse his bare feet. Someone passed them going down. He felt body warmth and a dampness in the air, but the face was hidden in the darkness.

The ascent continued endlessly. Then the spiral staircase came to an end. He caught sight of the first stars through a narrow doorway. The horizon where the sun had disappeared was a strip of green. Above this it whitened before an inky darkness spread from the middle of the evening sky like the sudden diffusion of smoke after an explosion. He took a step forward and then stopped. The railing around the narrow balcony did not even reach his knees. The gulf lured him, he did not know from which direction, up or down, towards the silvery dots in the darkness above him or the dim blobs of light strewn over the town below.

A white glare lit up the space at the foot of the tower, those sitting there rose and moved closer together at one end, a loudspeaker started to chatter.

He bent his knees slightly and edged back through the doorway. He was sweating copiously. There was a push from behind. He went out on to the balcony again. His body swayed uncontrollably as if he had lost the ability to keep balance, he had no hold over himself, sobs and cries clutched each other in his throat, panic threatened. He inched back towards the doorway, he dared not turn his back on the abyss nor look down into it, he tried to see his own bare feet but they were too far down in the darkness. Someone pulled at him again.

At the doorway he was pushed back, the staircase was full of people, they wanted to walk around the spire and elbowed their way forward. He could not move, they pushed and shouted, their eyes flashing weirdly. He uttered a sound, he did not know what language it was, and stretched out his hands as if already clutching at something in his fall. One of the white-clad figures climbed up on the rail, he turned towards Thomas, his mouth opened in a grin, then he took a step backwards into empty space and in a whirl of loosely flapping garments plummeted towards the ground far below. Thomas closed his eyes and screamed in terror. It seemed to him that the scream lasted an eternity and that the darkness around him was so total that it must be he himself who had jumped.

When he opened his eyes again all was as before. From below the voice of the loudspeaker rose up to him, the white-clad figures stood at the far end of the square, he stared out over the rail, there was nothing at the foot of the tower.

He was alone on the balcony. He looked up at the first stars. He could hear the ticking of the seconds, slowly the minutes, hours, days and years came back to him, for a moment they had gone away and he had stared across an abyss that he imagined had nothing to do with the distance between the spire and the ground far below. He had seen a *doppelgänger* who was always lying in wait for him, the *doppelgänger* had jumped in the hope that he would follow. That was all he knew, for a moment he had seen himself there at the top of the tower in a leap from which no one could call him back.

George waited down in the square. Beside him stood an elderly man wearing an embroidered skullcap, a long white beard flowing down his chest. He looked at Thomas inquisitively and coughed. A pink tongue appeared in his beard.

'What country?' he asked when the paroxysm of coughing was over.

Thomas told him.

The old man looked pleased. 'Ahhh,' he said with a long drawn-out sound that again showed his mouth pinkly in the beard, 'good country, milk products, many cows.'

He stared hard at Thomas expecting praise for his knowledge. Thomas smiled faintly. A crowd of white-clad figures had gathered around them. The old man turned to the assembly.

'Milk products, many cows,' he lectured.

'Milk products, milk products,' the words were repeated among the flock of listeners.

At that moment Thomas fainted.

When he came to himself again the old man was squatting beside him.

'The boy must eat.' He slapped his stomach and looked at George reproachfully. 'Not good, not good.'

Thomas got to his feet, he stood drooping in the midst of the crowd, embarrassed at the attention he was causing.

The old man took his arm and led him down the steps into the street. The crowd followed chattering loudly, excited by the spectacle. Their numbers swelled in the narrow street. The words milk products were repeated over and over. It was no longer the old man leading him, he was propelled by the massed bodies carrying him along.

He was pushed into an eating place. Small tables crowded close together, no wall separated the room from the street, outside the crowd stood there gaping. He looked round for George but could not see him. The old man pushed him down on to a chair and shouted an order.

A fat man with oiled hair and mutton-chop whiskers

placed a bowl in front of him. The man stood in front of the table, his hands at his sides, as if awaiting the result of an experiment. He said something to the old man while he continued to stare at Thomas.

Thomas looked at the bowl.

'Eat, eat,' commanded the old man.

Thomas did not react.

The old man shouted another order. The fat man left his observation post for a moment and came back with a spoon. The old man put the spoon in Thomas's hand. His wrinkled old man's hand felt dry as wood.

'Eat, eat!' The old man stabbed at Thomas with a pointed finger. The fat man with the moustache leaned encouragingly over the table.

Thomas lifted the spoon to his mouth. The spices burned his throat. He chewed. His teeth crunched on a fragment of bone.

'Chicken?'

'Yes, yes,' the old man wagged his head in assent.

There was nothing left of the chicken but bones, the meat had been burned away by the spices. He felt as if a stranger was rummaging in his mouth with a dirty finger.

He spat out the bone into the bowl and pushed the food away. He did not look up. He was afraid they would see the tears in his eyes. He felt like crying out but did not dare. The old man clapped his hands and gave a fresh order. A discussion broke out among the crowd in the street. The waiter brought a glass of white liquid and placed it before Thomas.

Thomas tasted it cautiously. He dared not do otherwise. It was sour milk.

'Milk product, milk product,' chanted the old man excitedly.

'Milk product, milk product,' the crowd took up the refrain as if it was the term for a species that included Thomas.

He was an animal in a cage.

Everything closed in on him. His tongue lay in his mouth like the damp larva of a parasite.

In the middle of the wall of humanity he caught sight of George. His eyes were filled with the same merciless inquisitiveness as the rest.

9

The wooden walls were green. There was no more than an arm's length between the two beds, that was the extent of the whole space. The room was nothing but a box of boards. At the height of a couple of metres a layer of wire netting was fixed across it, higher up the structure ended in a ceiling whose dimensions showed that the box was situated in a big room, a hum of voices floated up there.

They had been staying there for a day or two, and the resemblance to a prison had struck him the moment they walked down the narrow corridor of green-painted planks, in which the doors to the rooms had only a couple of metres between them.

High up on a wall behind the rooms his gaze caught a clockface that shone white in the half-darkness of the vast space. It must be early afternoon. He lay down on the bed and lost himself in watching the hands, moving with springy little jerks, two sharp arrows ready to be shot out into space and yet nailed to a clock that would never let them escape from the bowstring.

He remembered a riddle from his childhood: What is it that goes and goes and never gets any further? It was always the same old lady who asked him the riddle and each time the answer was the same: it was time, and she pointed to the clock that hung on the wall between two windows looking out to the street, and the clock had been the same as the one he looked at now, with Roman numerals and black arrows behind a glass plate, in a wooden casing reminiscent of the façade of a Greek temple. The dark varnished furniture was closely crowded in her living-room, the wallpower was yellow with tobacco smoke, the only remaining trace left of a departed spouse. There were photographs everywhere, buttoned-up men and women whose features were blurred by the light, only the eyes were clearly marked, transformed into dark holes like a warning of the death that had long since struck down all these people from another age.

It was as if the portraits on the walls and the heavy furniture were also a part of the clock and its unvarying ticking, that movement that was yet no movement, that going that was yet no more than the hamster running round the treadmill.

Every time the old lady posed the riddle of the eternally unavailing movement of time he felt his body tense. He pretended to be stupid and incapable of answering.

He looked at the bed next to his. George's travel bag lay on top of the unmade bed. He didn't recall the Indian leaving the room. He must have slept for a long time. His body felt black and blue as if he had influenza. He shut his eyes and opened them again. The hands on the white clock-face pursued their endless round.

He decided to wash his face. He went out to the bathroom, filled a brass jar from the watertank and splashed water over his head.

When he was back in the room he felt restless. He

went out into the corridor, put the padlock on the door and locked it. Then he remembered his money, it was unwise to leave it in the hotel room, and he re-entered the room straight away.

He picked up the pillow. The money should be under it, in a stomach belt he always wore under his clothes. The thick wad of notes from the black money market made him bulge as if he was pregnant with the riches of the whole of his own continent. At night after the light was put out he hid the belt under the pillow. He had not been able to decide whether it was a sensible or a childish security measure before one evening when he saw George do the same with his purse. 'It's not that I think you will rob me,' the Indian had said. After that Thomas himself had started to hide his belt even before the light was extinguished, and George had looked at him benevolently, like the teacher of a bright pupil.

Now the belt had gone.

He stood with the pillow in his hand staring at the blank sheet. Then he threw down the pillow, with a jerk he tore the sheet from the bed. The stained mattress came in sight. He pulled the bed away from the wall expecting to hear the thump when the belt struck the floor.

Nothing happened.

He kneeled down and looked first under one bed, then the other. He ran his hands over the dirty floor as if he no longer trusted his own eyes. He stood up again and stared at George's bed.

Then he picked up the Indian's pillow.

Energy had already forsaken his movements, conscious-ness of the uselessness of his search washed through his body. He sat down on the hard mattress with a bump and felt a throbbing in his temples. The sentence 'I've been robbed' hardly managed to formulate itself before it was pushed away again by a swarm of other thoughts that streamed in like white blood corpuscles to a wound when an infection needs to be withstood.

George's bag was on his bed. That meant that George was still there. Not in the room, but somewhere else, his friend and travelling companion, as a guarantee that the unthinkable had not suddenly happened.

Where George was now, and where his own money was, was impossible to explain. He, Thomas, could not explain it. But there was an explanation.

He was sure of it.

At that moment his faith in the Indian came upon him, he had not thought of George like this before, he had seen their journey as a practical arrangement, a temporary exchange of mutual convenience, which literally only took place between two railway stations and then was ended. Now he remembered their conversation that evening when George had talked about his first lover, and his own need to confide in someone. No one had ever listened to him like George. He had dared to completely reveal himself, and George had touched him.

That was the decisive thing.

His faith in George brooked no argument, it came like a sudden cleansing that ran through his body.

He felt the pressure in his temples recede and rose from his collapsed position on the bed.

George would come back.

He settled down to wait. After a while he lost patience

again and went out into the street after again turning the key in the padlock. He stood for a couple of minutes in the hotel entrance and then began to walk to and fro.

On the opposite pavement he caught sight of a man in a white nylon shirt. The distance blurred the man's face, but he had a broad forehead with black hair combed back. Thomas ran across the street, behind an ox-cart with big jolting wooden wheels, a rickshaw wallah shouted at him, then he was across. He could not see the man anywhere, he rose on tiptoe and saw the white back a long way ahead. He started to run again and caught up with him, at the last moment too shy to slap the man on the shoulder. It was not George, he had not made himself known before he saw it, the other man had heavier features, he kept in step with him for a while, seized with the idea that it was actually George, and that he could not distinguish one Indian from another. Then disappointment got the upper hand and he came to a halt.

Aggrieved, he looked at the passing crowds as if at some composite life form with its own independent will that had consciously deprived him of the appearance of the face he longed so much to see.

He felt the need for refreshment and went up to a booth to ask for a glass of tea. He had already given his order when he remembered his missing money. His heart started to hammer. A moment earlier the whole thing had been a question of George's reappearance. Now he saw himself thirsting with no money and every barrier between him and the crowd in the street breaking down. He could end up like one of those who slept in the street.

As that thought ran through his mind he turned round and ran back to the hotel.

He lay down on his bed and folded his hands on his chest. He must keep calm until George came back.

And George would come.

He stared tensely at the clock hands and tried to control his terror.

He managed to lie on the bed with his hands folded on his chest for several hours. Then he got up to go out into the street again.

It was late afternoon, dusk was approaching.

The hotel was on a corner where three streets met. Expectation of the coolness the darkness would bring had already increased the volume of traffic. At the crossroads a massive tangle had built up of people and animals, ox-carts and cycle rickshaws, they had come streaming down the streets and were now hopelessly locked together. Nothing moved. The wallahs sat with their bodies leaning on their handlebars, veins swelling on tensed hands and up skinny arms. A man who had been trying to cross the street stood stock still while a sudden gust of wind flapped the white garment he wore. The oxen bowed their heads. The bulky coachwork of a bus reared up in the red evening light like a distant cliff in a slowly eroding desert.

It seemed to Thomas that at that moment there was not a sound to be heard here. The silence filled him with respect. He had once seen a dog get tangled up in its lead. Every movement it made to free itself made things worse. Finally it gave up and stood completely still with an expression beyond even patience and resignation. It had emptied its animal soul of every restless impulse and instead filled it with philosophical indifference to fate.

He had the feeling that he could walk around among the people sitting there paralyzed and locked into the centre of the chaos at the crossroads. He could have looked into their faces and they would not have stared back, he could have laid his hand on their arms and they would not have felt it, he could have stroked the sweaty flanks of the oxen and they would not have so much as turned their heavy heads.

He was totally alone.

He stood there just as unmoving as the petrified figures in the street in front of him, he did not even lift an arm or utter a whisper.

This lasted for only a moment. Or it did not happen at all.

Then a cry arose from the street, then the cycle bells began to ring, then the oxen put their feet down into the dust and heaved the heavy carts into motion again, then came the sound of an engine that made the coachwork of the bus vibrate, then the man crossing the street gathered his garments around him and went on.

For a moment he had believed they would stand there for ever, now instead he saw how they pressed forward centimetre by centimetre, towards each other, past each other, centimetre by centimetre the stream passing along the street would move, it would continue like that the whole time, the street would never stay the same.

In so enormous a country with its hundreds and yet more hundreds of millions of people, two people would never meet more than once. For here the streets were like rivers, the name stayed the same, but you could never pass through the same river twice. Not even chance could bring that about. To meet again you would have to search for each other.

And he felt with great certainty, while the mass of humanity in the streets around him moved forward centimetre by centimetre: that no one was looking for him here.

He went back to the hotel room.

George's bag was still on the bed. He had not touched it, not even when he was most desperately searching for his lost money. It had merely lain there as a guarantee that George was still there and that therefore everything was as it should be. Now he went straight to the bag and turned it upside-down.

A sheet of paper fell out, nothing else.

For a moment he thought the paper might have something to do with him, that perhaps it was a letter or some kind of explanation for George's disappearance. Then he rejected the idea. If George had wanted to leave him a message he would have put it somewhere where it would be seen. He did not feel any guilt over looking at George's bag, it seemed rather as if the bag had belonged to someone who had died and he was free to do with it what he liked.

He picked up the piece of paper. It was covered with Hindi letters. He would never be able to read what it said.

When he realized this he lay down on his bed with his hands folded on his chest. He felt an inexplicable peace.

After a short while he fell asleep. When he woke up again he could see from the clock that it must be morning. It was just before six o'clock. He felt completely rested.

He rose and smoothed out the sheet. He packed his rucksack and left the room, leaving George's bag where it was. At the reception he sat down on a chair.

'I have been robbed,' he said, 'I can't pay my bill.'

10

He was out in the street.

He could hear the hotel guests laughing inside, they had shared out the contents of his rucksack among themselves and in payment handed him a small bundle of rupees. He did not know whether they were laughing at him. He did not care.

He felt the empty rucksack flapping against his calf. It had the same lightness he felt in his body. As if he had emptied himself.

It was the same peace he had felt as he went to sleep, his hands folded on his chest. He did not want to lose that.

It was George who had saved him from kicking a child. And it was George who had struck another human being on the back with his flat hand, as if the other were merely an animal. There was the touch, the hand on his knee. And there was the theft.

He did not know who George was.

Now he was turning his back on it all and going away.

He thought of the sculptor creating his sculpture by taking away and taking away.

He had not eaten for two days.

He could feel it. That was where the lightness lay. In the empty rucksack. In the empty stomach. In this body where the skin settled closer and closer to the bones.

The street slowly glided past him. The dust stirred up by the feet of the pedestrians hovered in the air like mist.

He spat out a grain of dust that had lodged in his mouth.

11

The horse trotted with its legs raised so high it seemed about to move into a gallop. It tossed its head impatiently, a red tassel nodded between the alertly pricked ears. There was a charged power about its movements, and the sight of the muscles working under the sweat-glossy skin took him out of his hypnotic trance for a moment.

The excitement of the horse was infectious, it seemed to send a convulsive jolt through the densely flowing mass of humanity. While the horse, which was harnessed to a canopied vehicle, went past with hoofs clattering, Thomas lurched uncomfortably to and fro in the rickshaw.

The cycle rickshaw bumped along on its hard tyres. The saddle creaked under the wallah's efforts. His bare feet kicked at the pedals.

The wallah turned round and gave him a weak grin.

They turned off the wide street and entered a labyrinth of narrow alleyways. The pedestrians pressed closer and the temperature seemed to escalate. Several times the rickshaw was brought to a halt by the crowd. Then they were through. The streets widened out again and the houses grew lower. They were coming into a kind of suburb, the rickshaw lurched wildly, there was no tarmac on the road, it was full of potholes and mounds. There was no street lighting, only fires burning at intervals along the roadside. The firelight flickered on prone and seated figures. Most were enveloped in big shawls as if expecting a very cold night. The houses behind them looked ruinous. Straw mats were piled up in a chaotic jumble, an opening could be by chance or a door, the play of the flames created unexpected shadows everywhere.

The holes in the road grew worse. Piles of earth lay beside them. There did not seem to be any plan for the digging, some holes were in the middle of the road, others beside the houses.

They stopped in front of a brick-built house two or three storeys high, it was difficult to see in the darkness. In the light of the fires it looked as if it had once been yellow, now black shadows of rot and mould spread up the walls. The windows were boarded up, surrounded by damp the planks seemed grey and dry, like fossils of felled trees from a petrified forest. Once woodworms had gnawed their way through the living wood, now their tunnels were laid bare like the veins in a piece of butchered flesh.

A crowd that grew bigger by the minute pushed around the rickshaw. They were silent, their faces hidden in the shadow of the shawls pulled down low over their foreheads.

Thomas stood still for a moment, uncertain of his own desire to go on with this. Then the wallah took the decision for him and pedalled off. The men stepped aside to let the cycle through. The circle closed again and they came nearer. The fires flickered behind them, their bodies flowed together into a multi-headed animal whose silhouette grew until it concealed the lights behind it.

A small man in dirty shorts and open-necked shirt

appeared in the doorway. He grimaced encouragingly and beckoned to Thomas. The grimace of welcome stayed on his face as he closed the door behind them unexpectedly quickly. With his hand he indicated a stairwell leading up into thick darkness. His mouth opened soundlessly in a toothless slit which made his jaw split in two so he looked like a little sick frog.

On the first floor he led the way along a dark corridor. They entered a room where a dull bulb threw a yellowish light over walls covered with faded newspaper. A man lay stretched out on the floor staring at the ceiling with an absent gaze and resting his head on hands clasped behind his neck. Along the walls sat a hunched row of people, one with head on his breast as if he was asleep, another leaning his head against the wall staring at the ceiling with lifeless eyes and picking at an invisible wound on his knee with a slow hypnotic movement. They were all dressed in the same greyish-yellow shorts as the man who had opened the door. In the poor light you could not see whether the colour resulted from dirt deposited over a lengthy period, or was perhaps the actual colour of the material, a colour like that of old used sacks, which emphasized the lifelessness of the bodies hidden under the garments, and blended into the faded walls so the room took on an almost monochrome character from which the human presence would have to be deciphered like hidden patterns in a puzzle picture.

An immense beard spread down over the chest of one of the seated figures. It gave out a bluish light, as if the last remnants of life in the room had concentrated in the untamed growth of beard. Above it a narrow face stood out, the owner of the beard was still young, but already ravaged, with long vertical furrows down his sunken cheeks. His eyes were deepset beneath brows which grew as thickly as the beard. He looked at Thomas, and his eyes filled with piercing hostility. Then the expression faded like a drowning body relinquishing the effort to keep afloat, and the blind stare came back.

The manikin fetched a small pile of newspapers from a corner of the room and spread it on the floor in front of him. He pointed to the papers and Thomas lay down. Then he placed an empty jam jar under Thomas's head and showed him how he was to lie on his side with his temple resting on the jar.

He stretched out his hand. When Thomas did not react he took a rupee note from his shorts pocket and waved it about impatiently. He wanted Thomas to pay before he lay down beside him. He smiled into space, a vague meaningless smile directed at no one and meaning nothing, merely a contraction of the muscles beneath the loose skin of the little frog cranium.

They lay like two reflections of each other, their heads slightly raised, resting on the jam jar, and their arms bent underneath them to cushion them from the hard floor. Their hips formed a soft almost feminine curve. There was certainly nothing feminine about the pathetic frog face of the manikin, his wasted chest or the loose skin that hung in little empty bags beneath his sharp elbows. All the same, there was an intimacy in the situation not unlike that between man and woman.

The other began to prepare the opium pipe. The pipe was a long sturdy tube in the middle of which was a pipe bowl. Instead of an opening this had a row of small holes, almost like a flue. Some black oily liquid was spread over the bowl. This was the opium, which a moment before had been melted over an oil lamp. The Indian tested it by taking a pull. The smoke smelt sweet and sickly. Then with a lazily amicable movement he handed the pipe to Thomas.

At the first pull Thomas coughed. The physical contact of the sweet aroma with his throat and windpipe changed it into a gentle, almost healing touch. But he was so unaccustomed to smoking that his lungs contracted gaspingly as he struggled to draw in the smoke. The man looked at him disapprovingly, jolted out of his sleepy routine. He took the pipe from Thomas. His frog mouth closed around the mouthpiece, the slack lips gripped it as he demonstrated the technique. He held the smoke inside himself with an expression that again grew absent, then he directed an astonishing amount of smoke into the well-aimed streams of the practised smokers.

The Indian spread more of the oily opium over the pipe bowl and handed the pipe to Thomas with an encouraging movement. This time it went better. He felt the sweet smoke in his windpipe and struggled to hold it inside. Then he exhaled it slowly in a great well-controlled cone-shaped cloud. He handed the man another rupee note.

With the same slow languishing movement as before, the recumbent figure beside him prepared the next pipe.

When Thomas had smoked the second pipe he stretched himself out flat on the floor and closed his eyes. Some time passed before anything happened. He felt it was odd to lie with closed eyes and opened them again. The floor was covered with recumbent bodies like his own. The opium man had gone to lie down beside a new client. The dim light in the ceiling could not hide the dilapidation and dirt in the grubby yellow room. He had seen the colour of sick people suffering from inflammation of the liver. That was what the room looked like.

He had been lying there for a while when he noticed the diarrhoea, the same contraction of the gut system he had come to know so well on his journey. It was always accompanied by a lassitude which made him go weak at the knees and feel indifferent to each wave of dizziness as if it was his urge for self-preservation rather than his sphincter that had given way, and the need for evacuation was actually total and did not merely concern the bowels but the whole of his being, in a temptation to give in completely, as if the string that held him upright would grow slack and melt away so that he became one with the earth and let it devour him like the turbid liquid that came splashing out of him in the diarrhoea.

He got reluctantly to his feet. With uncoordinated halting movements and stiff knees he went out of a door and down a dark corridor. The corridor took a turn, he felt his way along the wall with his hand and came to an opening like a dense gloom in the darkness of the corridor. He could not see anything but the stench told him that there must be a toilet inside.

The floor gave under his feet like damp clay. He had not realized his feet were bare. He pulled down his trousers slowly. They were Indian and as wide as pyjama trousers, with just a cord round the waist. It came streaming out of him, almost like a welling spring and without giving him the feeling of being invaded by an alien element which he usually felt with diarrhoea. Nor was there any of the sharp

85

smarting in the sensitive area around his anus which was its usual accompaniment. It was almost a pleasure to empty himself, as if he was giving something to the bowl beneath him and quenching a thirst in the damp absorbent clay.

When he straightened up he slipped and one foot landed in the contents of the sunken pan. It was too firm to be his own. He noted that the disgust which momentarily filled him at contact with a stranger's excretion was merely a habit-determined reflex. He felt no nausea and his diaphragm did not start to contract as it usually did with a strange sour taste or far less unpleasant odour. He found the tap at floor level and let it run, that was a reflex too, he was in no hurry to wash the sticky shit from his foot, it was merely as a polite acknowledgement of the habits of his upbringing that he cleaned himself.

He felt no desire to leave the small black cubby hole with its concentrated stench.

He stood there for a while, he did not know how long, holding up his trousers with one hand without tying the cord while he allowed his thoughts to flow slowly through him. He let them go with a little plop, like raindrops striking the surface of the sea. His brain was a cloud, a moment's concentration of dampness and warmth. It dripped from him in a drizzle of sentences and single words dissolving into fractions of themselves.

Thomas.

His own name. He had to laugh at the uselessness of trying to spell out the infinity that was a name.

He drifted along the corridor, incapable of orienting himself, he could not hold on to the idea that the corridor took a bend but just stared, as if he had come to the end of a blind alley. Then he turned round and drifted back the way he had come. Again he passed the stinking toilet, now he did not need it, he had to go on. Further along the darkness was broken by a beam of light on the floor. He went into it and stood bathing his feet in the light. The wall beside him had pulled back, it made a fold and pushed the blackness away. He stared at a small flame. It pulsed, and the space drew air around it, a constant breathing in and out of light and darkness. He could clearly hear the faint breathing emerging from the small body of light of the flame.

He was standing in the doorway of a room. Only now did he realize it. An oil lamp was burning on the floor, it was a wick stuck in a brown bottle, its irregular flame now sent the darkness up the walls, now allowed it to possess the room again. At the end of the room was a bed with a plaited rope bedstead. He caught sight of a figure lying there, looking at him with one hand beneath its head. The hair was pinned up in an intricate style. The nose was strong and curved, the eyes, very slightly crossed, gave the face a formidable symmetry. The upper part of the body was naked, in the light of the flame the skin gleamed like gold, the waist was narrow but beneath a loose voluminous garment Thomas glimpsed hips of an overwhelming voluptuousness.

A slim hand beckoned him closer, only the index and little fingers were raised, the others lay folded over the palm, the studied movement resembled the beginning of a dance. Thomas went into the room. The light was a fluid he swam in. He came to a halt in front of the bed. The woman moved herself nearer the wall with a gracefully inviting gesture, with the tips of thumb and little finger lightly touching each other, at the same time dropping her wrist.

Thomas lay down beside her, the mattress was so narrow they had to lie breast to breast, both with hand beneath head. The woman's breast was hard and elastic, as if full of muscles, he felt the warmth of her body through her clothes.

They lay there for a while without moving. At such close quarters the woman's face seemed to Thomas to be immensely big. He became totally absorbed in studying it, as if he were a space probe circling a planet. That was precisely how he observed it, as if the symmetrical features were continents and oceans he flew over with his gaze. A caste mark shone on her forehead. The rainbow-coloured film over the eye swam in yellow. He could not penetrate into that eye any more than he could see through the shining skin of the face. It was like a goat's eye or a crocodile's when in a slow sideways movement the eyelid slid into place. He was not staring into another world when he looked into the recumbent woman's eyes. He was not staring into any world, merely at a damply glistening surface of faintly phosphorescent patterns and shadowy patches.

He let his hand follow the lines of the perfect body in a great abstract ecstasy. He felt the strange skin under his fingertips and at the same time a warmth against his own when their hands searched for each other on mutual impulse. He felt his existence found its place here, like a slowly rolling line between two points of contact. They reached each other's hips at the same moment, as if the symmetry in their position controlled the direction of their movements. His penis was in the woman's hand, he did not know if it was hard or not, it seemed rather as if penis and hand were two animals at rest beside each other. His own hand travelled down the generous curve of the hip, the garment that had covered the lower part of the woman's body slipped away, and he felt a swelling bulge of flesh against his palm. He looked down without surprise, his gaze merely continuing the scanning of the room he had begun earlier as he walked towards the bed, and which his hand had continued. Under the opulent arch of the hip was an organ like his own, there was no difference, without protest he accepted the mysterious reflection of himself which the woman's body presented, it was like touching his own body, and yet it was another being's warmth he found in his palm. In the body facing him there was nothing that opened to receive him, no penetration or union was possible, they merely lay side by side and it was as if by being so like him the woman made him a part of her untouchableness.

When he leaned over her to take her hard breast into his mouth he thought he was about to suckle at eternity.

He closed his eyes and felt earth in his mouth.

There were feet around him with deep furrows in the horny skin of the soles and yellow nails that dug into dark flesh.

Gravel scratched his cheek.

He lay on the ground, the world tasted of dust. He had it in his mouth.

He spat and rose abruptly.

Dark figures bent down over him, their faces hidden and shadowed by their shawls. He put a hand on the chest of one, the figure stepped back with a mildness that neutralized the push. His agitation increased. He began to shout, his own words were incomprehensible to him, perhaps they were merely fractions of words. He elbowed his way through the crowd still shouting. No one resisted him as he shoved, and yet it seemed as if he was getting nowhere, an endless swarm of heads pressed around him. He felt he was walking through fluid rubber, that enraged him too, he was seized with celestial impatience, filled with a godlike haste, demanding to reach the stars before night. He saw them drifting away in the sky above him, torn from their moorings by the same storm that had seized him. There was darkness over him and within him, he felt the wild dance of entrails in his body. Nothing but a thin dividing wall enclosed them, soon the skin would burst like tent canvas under the pressure of the gale and the bloody organs untwine their wild growth among the tossing stars in a meeting of darkness with darkness.

Then he ran. He leapt over the piles of earth in the road, tumbled into a hole and got to his feet again, crossed mountains and valleys, now he was traversing continents in the midst of the mud.

He had been running a long time, he did not know how long, people and houses rushed past him without variation, rooted to the earth, he alone was in movement, the taste of dust still reminded him of the life he once shared with the rest of humanity. He caught sight of the horse, it stood waiting for him at the end of a street, his old friend from the outward journey, its skin shone brightly, he saw straight through it to the expectant bones that longed for the winds from the stars and the vast breath that blew through the world of the paralysed. Only he and it noticed it, they were quite alone with the rushing wind, and their tails swept in fellowship over the congealed earth. Taking great leaps he drew nearer and with an extra long and reckless leap he was up on the seat and had kicked the driver down on the ground. The horse needed no command, it already knew him and at once felt liberated by his presence. It started off through the streets at a gallop. He clutched the seat laughing, aware only of the play of muscles beneath the horse's sweat-dripping skin. He tore at his own clothes and felt his body running with sweat after the long sprint. His hands slid up and down through the wetness. He tried to find the muscles he saw in the horse.

In front of the hurtling animal the streets were empty. Sleepers lay in long rows on the pavements. The echoes of the hoofbeats among the houses were like ecstatic music to his ears, an awakening that moved over the world with him and the horse as heralds, and that was indeed the effect, all the time as they travelled a keelwater of heads rose up out of the sleeping rows, torn from slumber they gazed from their rags as witnesses to Thomas's triumphal progress. He and the horse galloped in an eternity along this avenue of dark faces.

A barrier rose up in front of them. The town, awakening, approached in a whirl of human bodies, ringing cycles and roaring lurching buses, a floodwave conjured up by the day, foaming forcefully with a life like the fish caught in the wave rolling towards land, the horse and Thomas were drawn towards it into the red light of the morning, they had run for so long they drove each other on, still filled with the night, red against black, morning against the darkness that would not yield, the roar of the buses grew louder, the horse's hoofs were a sliding pile of timber, the air seemed full of flying foam, then the wave burst over them

91

in a chaos of pitching cycle-spokes and dented ripped metal plates, while open mouths gaped pink in silent screams like stranded fish. The horse's back cracked, the stretched skin split so flesh and bones rose into the air like a geyser, Thomas turned a somersault right over the smashed canopy, then he straightened out and like a white arrow shot up into the red morning sky where his body was sucked into the cloud-pump of blood and organs that rose slowly looping from the horse up into the night that now seemed only a shrinking inkblot far far away in the ever-brightening sky.

At last, at last released from the hard straitjacket of the skin.

12

At first he thought, They have broken through me, just as he would have thought, They have broken through the wall. A passage had been opened in his forehead, something would slip out, or something would slip in. He stood in front of a mirror. He had a fine thin gash just beneath his hairline, the blood oozed down towards one eyebrow all along the wound.

He had expected to see the blood hanging in the air in a little cloud of red, that was how he conceived the air, as a new, a fifth element, half fire, half water, so hot, so damp, the temperature of the air was the same as his body, so it had to be like that: like being in a world of fluid matter, inside himself.

He stared into the mirror again. The blood glistened, red and sticky, it continued its slow advance down towards his eyebrow, his forehead was covered with small waterdrops.

He returned to his room and lay down on the bed. Through the open door he could see into the room opposite. A man lay on his back with one arm beneath his head. He came to think of a fish waiting in a crevice on a coral reef. The feel of water filled his limbs.

The man looked up and caught sight of him. He

pointed to the wound in his forehead and started to grimace.

Thomas stood up and closed the door.

three

1

Last night I dreamed two dreams.

I dreamed the old Thomas came back.

In the first dream I was staying in a house under seige.
It was a tall white house. I was on the top floor. Outside
the sun shone. It was the middle of the day. I was with a
group of people, I've forgotten their faces. I had a machine
gun in my hands. It was my task to protect the others. I
knew the attack would come soon and that I would definitely
be killed. I was seized with acute fear, it came on like an
attack of cramp, and in my sleep I had the feeling of
throwing myself around in the bed and gasping, almost
woken by my own terror. Then the seizure was over and I
was completely calm, prepared to die. The room was filled
with golden afternoon light and I felt the happiness you
attain when you are reconciled to your destiny.

The wall behind us was covered with a large dark
painting, I cannot recall the theme, perhaps it is of no
importance. Suddenly we discovered a door in one corner
of the painting, it had been hidden behind thick layers of
varnish. Behind the door opening was a secret passage that
could lead us all to safety. Our enemy had not yet begun
to storm the house. The possibility of salvation was a miracu-
lous opportunity. I kept watch by the stairs while the others
vanished into the painting.

It was at that moment that I realized I did not want to change my resolve. I wanted to stay and die a death that was now useless and superfluous. I took up position in front of the painting and set myself to wait. After a while I heard them breaking into the house and ascending the stairs.

I awoke still full of the feeling of happiness.

Shortly afterwards I fell asleep again. It must have been approaching morning although it was not yet light. In the second dream I was going up in a balloon. I found myself on a wooden staging that surrounded the balloon and kept it in place. The balloon must have been enormous. I only saw its underside, it completely obscured the view as if I was under a roof. The wooden structure was very large too, as was the gondola.

At the crucial moment the balloon would not rise. The wooden structure and the gondola seemed to be built into each other in an impenetrable whole which kept the balloon fixed. The colours of the dream were very dark. It seemed as if the balloon would hang there hiding the sky instead of going up into it.

This time when I woke up it was with the feeling that my life was a failure.

While I was having breakfast I read through what I had written the previous day. It was the second time I had reached the same place and come to a stop.

The two dreams kept coming back.

Thomas could have dreamed the first one. In a way it was he who had dreamed it in me. But isn't it always like that? Who knows how old the dreamer is?

And might he also have acted like that outside the dream?

I think my answer is yes. He could have let himself be shot to no purpose, merely to enjoy the unsullied purity and consistency in an absurd action.

In the second dream he wants to punish me. It is my life he is mocking when the balloon will not lift. What I call maturity and presence of mind to him is immobility and cowardice. I know. He is inside me the whole time worrying away at me.

That is why I write.

I often think of the old saying that the child is father of the man. When I look at a picture of myself as a child I feel the tenderness and indulgence which must naturally affect an older and more experienced person at the sight of a child's unprotected and expectant face. And I feel the urge to protect although it is of course absurd when you think of the gulf of time that lies between us. But the most absurd part of all is that I and my ageing body sit on the lap of this child with the pure face, which I once was. Its experiences fill my horizon, what happened to it was decisive, it has given birth to me, I take up so little room beside it, it holds me in its hand, and even though it has not yet learned to walk, yet it is the child that leads me. I try to wrench myself out of its soft grasp. I am impatient for I know I shall die if I am a child for long.

But the child holds on.

We struggle with each other, Thomas and I. He won't let go. He is my past, my youth, what I was twenty years ago. And he is my father. For he decided for me. Now I am trying to alter his decisions.

I want to be Thomas's father.

That is why I write.

It is not true that one can see oneself in a photograph. Self-regard immediately turns one into someone else. In the same way one cannot write about oneself. But perhaps one can rewrite oneself.

It is like the dream. There is a hidden door in the painting and a secret passage behind it.

It's this that is my hope.

I was once on a journey, not the one to India, but another. My mother was ill and in hospital. We lived in a small town, and I had to get a bus to go and visit her. I wasn't very old and I always made the journey with an adult. I received a lot of attention from other adults at that time, but the attention only made me uneasy and suspicious. I was obsessed with longing for my mother and thought that everyone who was kind to me was trying to make me forget her. One day when I was wandering around in the streets, I got on the bus by myself. I didn't have any money on me but the bus driver must have recognized me, perhaps knew something of my history, for it was only a small town, anyway he let me stay. I realized then that I had managed to escape the kindly adults, I was quite alone, it was the first independent action of my life. I felt a kind of triumph, I can still recall it today.

The longing for my mother increased with each minute that passed and I impatiently observed every detail of the landscape. It was wintertime, and the bare trees alongside the highway shone black and wet. The clouds hung low, they seemed almost to lie upon the wintry black fields. I can still remember how the wooden mouldings of the bus and its imitation leather seats all gave out their own particular creak. I can even remember a faint smell of linoleum.

When I arrived at the hospital my mother had died. It might even have been that she died the same moment I arrived. They told me later how a nurse had found me. I stood beside my mother's bed staring at her face, almost buried in the pillow. It was not until then they discovered she was dead.

I don't remember anything myself. My memory had used up all its strength in the knife-sharp reproduction of the journey. Instead I have this strangely distorted memory that Thomas told to George. I stand in the door and watch a doctor dissecting my mother. The muscles and sinews of one arm are laid bare. He pulls a muscle with pincers and my mother's hand moves. I do not know why I chose this image as a replacement for the memory of my last moments with my mother.

For years I actually believed in the reality of this macabre recollection. Later I stopped believing it, but I could not forget it. Not many years ago I found out that the scene did really exist, only not in my life, but on the canvas of a famous painter. By chance I came upon a reproduction of Rembrandt's painting *The Anatomy Lesson* in a history of art. It is true that here it is a dead man, a criminal at that, who has been hanged. The doctor is surrounded by a number of spectators in various dramatic postures. But the position of the corpse, the doctor's face and the movement of his hand, and above all the dead person's own upstretched hand are precisely the same as in my recollection of the last meeting with my dead mother.

There is nothing mysterious about it. I must have seen a reproduction of *The Anatomy Lesson* as a child and later forgotten it because I had need of the theme in my own life.

When I think about the reasons for my journey to India I experience the same thing. I believe I myself wrote André Gide's words in *Fruits of the earth*, I hear them whispered in my ear by my youthful voice: 'What I sought along the roads was not so much an inn as my hunger.' Or Paul Nizan in *Adén Arabia*: 'I was twenty, and I will never allow anyone to assert that this is the most beautiful time of one's life. It is hard to learn one's role in the world.' And yet those are their words and not mine. I had never heard of those writers when I set off on my journey.

I had this urge that only comes in very early youth. I had read Knut Hamsun's *Hunger*. He had his Kristiania. I wanted to find mine. I remember Per Oscarsson's face in the film version of the novel, which I must have seen at the onset of my puberty. His cheeks are hollow, covered with a thin death's-head-like beard. When Ylajali returns his caress she gets a handful of loose hair. That was what I wanted: to have a hair loss caused by my rejection of the world.

There was one afternoon in India when I lay on the beach staring out over the sea until evening came and the breakers began to show a violet phosphorescence. I was watching the crabs. When the waves receded and the wet sand glittered in the reflection of the sunlight, they appeared out of holes in the sand. Their light bodies rocked in the high elegant suspension of their legs. With a sudden jerk they ran to meet the breakers and vanished in the foam. I saw how powerless they were compared with the strength of the wave. They slid along on their backs, their legs helpless as the wheels of a vehicle that stalls, then they were carried away in the rolling masses of water.

When the waves receded and a new one started to

break further out, the same thing happened again. An army of crabs emerged from the holes in the sand and rushed into the collapsing wall of water. I never saw them run back. I could not think what they were looking for in the waves.

It struck me that they lived in an element which was neither earth nor water. It was movement. They lived as if in trajectory, thrown up with legs in the air, beyond all balance.

I was looking for an image of myself.

There was a boy I used to talk with. He was small and frail but he radiated something older than himself. He had a responsiveness in his nature as of one who has learned to read others' wishes even before they are expressed. When he spoke his voice was soft as if he was offering a remedy for disease. He lived somewhere or other in the huge masses of stone in an Indian city. Early in the morning he opened a shop, he cleaned it, all day he ran errands, balancing a tray of tea across the street, cooking rice, baking chapati and pakoras, at night he was woken up just to pour out whisky. He was merely the hand that carried, turned, passed, cooked, poured. He was the invisible distance between the tea house and his master's guests, between the rice in the pan and the rice on the plate, between bottle and glass. The whole of his intelligence had developed in this state of dependence, he knew neither mother nor father, he knew only loneliness and humiliation, those were the materials with which he had to build his nature, and in the total workability of his deep dependence, in the midst of the endless flexibility of his existence, he had grown strong.

He lifted a hand and waved to me when we parted.

That was when I was in India and decided to shrink instead of grow.

I came back home.

I wandered around in India for a while with my empty rucksack and my little handful of rupee notes. Someone gathered me up and sent me home. I let them do it, just as I have so often before and since allowed others to take decisions for me.

When I was walking around with my empty rucksack I came to understand that in the deepest sense there was only one journey I was able to make.

Perhaps I had realized it a long time before, even when I stood looking at my mother.

But I didn't want to know about that sight. Others had to tell me about that.

Why have I twice come to a stop in the same place?

Thomas is alone in a hotel room. He has a wound in his forehead. And I can get no further. He won't let me. He closes the door on my story as if to indicate it is finished.

He is still inside me.

When I read what I have written I see that I never describe his appearance. I do not want to give him a face. I could easily do it, for after all he is myself. I could even invent one for him. Closed, perhaps, hidden behind hair, large features out of proportion to each other, the reshaping of the face in puberty not yet complete, spectacles, a shyness disguised as stand-offishness. Or short-haired with a totally open face, small undeveloped features, skin almost as clear as a girl's, innocent, with this frightful deadly yearning for purity written all over the face.

I could easily do it but I won't. I don't think he deserves

it. For it is a face he is talking about when he describes the line he drew in his childhood magazine through a series of numbered points. It is a face that he wants. That is why he travels in India.

And then he shuts the door on my story.

We really are fighting each other.

I happen to go into an Indian restaurant. I sit at the table and try to remember the taste of my youth. I run my eyes down the menu to see if I can rediscover one of the dishes I didn't want to know about then. The Indian waiters are friendly. They allow me to sit over the menu for a long time. I think they understand I've come here searching for other courses than culinary ones.

Once while I was sitting there I wrote this sentence on a serviette: 'I heard the noise of the colossal press of humanity in the streets of Bombay and New Delhi, and suddenly their countless voices joined together in a shout that awoke me.'

That is the dream, Thomas, that is how I would like to describe our journey.

A woman stands opposite me. Her eyes are very slightly crossed and with the hooked nose they give her face an expression of noble symmetry. She raises her index and little fingers, the other fingers are curled together in her palm. She looks as if she wants to dance.

She is a cardboard photostat advertising an airways firm. I always choose the table exactly opposite her.

You know her too. You chose her as your goddess that night in the opium cave. That is why our fight is so unequal. In her image you chose the untouchable. Then one is invincible.

How can I move someone who only wants to see the world as a mirror?

How absurd it is that I talk to you, Thomas, after all, you have become me, this half human at the foot of a colossal statue of a child, you who have shut the door behind you in your temple and locked me in with you.

I do not remember anything.

I do not recognize the names of food when I read the menu. On the map of India I cannot rediscover the towns I once visited.

I must write it all over again. But Thomas writes with me. And his weapon is oblivion and the terror I still feel for life, the terror he gave me.

The first page of my story. Thomas and the beggar boy. That is Thomas and me too. How I do long to let him feel my boot.

Once only do I let him see himself. It is at the summit of the minaret. He stands there midway between the lights that are lit in the town below him, and the stars that are lit in the sky above him. I can feel it: he wants to fall upwards. That is youth when it is most self-destructive and dangerous to itself: when it desires the absolute. Then I let a man step up on to the balustrade and throw himself down from the top of the minaret. Thomas may have a presentiment, but he misunderstands: it is his *doppelgänger*. I want to show him that we can only fall downwards. We have to obey the law of gravity. Don't most of our wrinkles point down towards the earth? Isn't this the answer to the riddle that calls itself time and the inevitable law of our ageing, that the earth pulls at us from our first step, and that life is nothing more than a little ironical game the law of gravity is playing with itself? I want to show him that law, he must adapt himself to it, the frightful duality of growth and maturity, that makes us decay even as we grow.

But he won't see it.

I offer him a bowl of food. He presses his lips together.

I give him a glass of milk. He thinks it is sour. He doesn't believe he belongs to this earth.

I show him that the stream of humanity in the street moves, centimetre by centimetre, for that is life's speed, I know that now. Only here can he belong, at this walking pace. But he turns his back on it all and walks away.

I give him dust in the mouth.

It is the only teaching I know.

He spits.

I allow him to run the line out and call it an opium orgy. Then, at the crucial moment when he believes he is going to suckle at eternity, I again give him earth in the mouth.

He rises and goes up to heaven.

There we are, locked together. Thomas and I.

107

2

I fantasized once, Thomas, that the whole of humanity had one common cemetery, like the elephants. It was a place on earth we travelled to and lay down in when we were about to die.

Then the riddle of time would be solved. It was only the clock hands that turned and turned without getting anywhere.

Not we.

Twice I gave you earth in the mouth.

The third time you will not be able to elude it.

Or shall I once more resume my story and let you stand in the doorway, with everything still in the balance, with life still in your hands?